FUJINO O

ILLUSTRATION BY
KIYOTAKA H

CHARACT
SUZUHITO

Like a
he tirele
worl
digg
his h
almost
though
de
hims
possess
hir

Is it WRONG
to TRY to
PiCK UP GIRLS
iN A DUNGEON?
ON THE
SIDE

Sword
Oratoria

CONTENTS

PROLOGUE   ♦ Villains 001

CHAPTER 1   ♦ Orario Now 007

CHAPTER 2   ♦ Dungeon Trap 035

CHAPTER 3   ♦ Feast of the Dead 073

CHAPTER 4   ♦ The Sword's Wind Calls 109

CHAPTER 5   ♦ Battle of Tears 171

EPILOGUE   ♦ To Be Yearned After 207

AIZ WALLENSTEIN:
A Level 6 adventurer and Orario's strongest swordswoman. A human girl of *Loki Familia*.

LEENE ARSHE:
A human supporter, healer, and member of *Loki Familia*.

TIONA HYRUTE:
An Amazon and first-tier adventurer. Tione's younger twin sister.

ANAKITY AUTUMN:
A catgirl and member of *Loki Familia*. Everyone calls her "Aki."

FILVIS CHALLIA:
Magic swordswoman, member of *Dionysus Familia*.

TIONE HYRUTE:
The elder of the two Amazonian sisters and a member of *Loki Familia*.

LEFIYA VIRIDIS:
An elven magic user who deeply admires Aiz.

© Kiyotaka Haimura

"C—...Captaaaaaaaaaaaaaaaaaaaaaaaaaaaaaaain!"

RAUL NORD:
A human member of *Loki Familia*'s reserve forces.

FINN DEIMNE:
The prum captain and glue of *Loki Familia*.

LEVIS:
A creature in relentless pursuit of Aiz.

"Die."

© Kiyotaka Haimura

"Seems like you're gettin' the hang of this whole high-and-mighty bit, hmm?"

"Hardly. More like gettin' a crick in the neck!"

Again and again, Thanatos's name rang through the hall, reverberating against the rock and stone.

THANATOS:
The god of death and patron deity of *Thanatos Familia*.

VALLETTA GREDE:
A human woman and member of *Thanatos Familia*. Seems to have some connection to Finn…?

VOLUME 7

FUJINO OMORI

ILLUSTRATION BY
KIYOTAKA HAIMURA

CHARACTER DESIGN BY
SUZUHITO YASUDA

YEN ON

NEW YORK

IS IT WRONG TO TRY TO PICK UP GIRLS IN A DUNGEON?
ON THE SIDE: SWORD ORATORIA, Volume 7
FUJINO OMORI

Translation by Liv Sommerlot
Cover art by Kiyotaka Haimura

DUNGEON NI DEAI WO MOTOMERU NO WA MACHIGATTEIRUDAROUKA GAIDEN SWORD ORATORIA vol. 7
Copyright © 2016 Fujino Omori
Illustration copyright © Kiyotaka Haimura
Original Character Design © Suzuhito Yasuda
All rights reserved.
Original Japanese edition published in 2016 by SB Creative Corp.
This English edition is published by arrangement with SB Creative Corp., Tokyo, in care of Tuttle-Mori Agency, Inc., Tokyo.

English translation © 2018 by Yen Press, LLC

Yen On
1290 Avenue of the Americas
New York, NY 10104

Visit us at yenpress.com
facebook.com/yenpress
twitter.com/yenpress
yenpress.tumblr.com
instagram.com/yenpress

First Yen On Edition: October 2018

Yen On is an imprint of Yen Press, LLC.
The Yen On name and logo are trademarks of Yen Press, LLC.

Library of Congress Cataloging-in-Publication Data
Names: Ōmori, Fujino, author. | Haimura, Kiyotaka, 1973– illustrator. | Yasuda, Suzuhito, designer.
Title: Is it wrong to try to pick up girls in a dungeon? on the side: sword oratoria / story by Fujino Omori; illustration by Kiyotaka Haimura; original design by Suzuhito Yasuda.
Other titles: Danjon ni deai wo motomeru no wa machigatteirudarouka gaiden sword oratoria. English.
Description: New York, NY: Yen On, 2016– | Series: Is it wrong to try to pick up girls in a dungeon? on the side: sword oratoria
Identifiers: LCCN 2016023729 | ISBN 9780316315333 (v. 1 : pbk.) | ISBN 9780316318167 (v. 2 : pbk.) | ISBN 9780316318181 (v. 3 : pbk.) | ISBN 9780316318228 (v. 4 : pbk.) | ISBN 9780316442503 (v. 5 : pbk.) | ISBN 9780316442527 (v. 6 : pbk.) | ISBN 9781975302863 (v. 7 : pbk.)
Subjects: CYAC: Fantasy.
Classification: LCC PZ7.1.O54 Isg 2016 | DDC [Fic]—dc23
LC record available at https://lccn.loc.gov/2016023729

ISBNs: 978-1-9753-0286-3 (paperback)
978-1-9753-0287-0 (ebook)

1 3 5 7 9 10 8 6 4 2

LSC-C

Printed in the United States of America

VOLUME 7

FUJINO OMORI

ILLUSTRATION BY **KIYOTAKA HAIMURA**
CHARACTER DESIGN BY **SUZUHITO YASUDA**

Villains

Гэта казка іншага сям'і,

злыдні

A mass of candles flickered in the subterranean chamber.

The stone hall was replete with robed figures wearing bands around their foreheads, their mouths hidden beneath folds of cloth. It was a sight undeniably reminiscent of an underground organization or arcane religious sect.

Though the air was heavy with a solemn silence, the depths of every eye present were aflame with passion.

It was a peculiar zeal, nestled into the stillness.

"My Lord, a new sister is here to ask for your benediction. Anoint her with your blessing," a man said, his robes a different hue to designate his higher level.

The hall consisted of a simple stone room, yet it was decorated like a sacred altar. The wall at the room's center bore the crest of the patron deity's familia—a heart of iron and bronze coupled with a single black wing, evocative of the reaper's scythe.

Kneeling before the altar was a beautiful elven maiden clad in naught but a robe. As the man raised his voice, the god himself appeared before her.

He was utterly gorgeous, radiating decadence and charm. Long silken hair like a woman's flowed down his back in a river of deep purple, and his towering frame, shrouded in tattered black robes, was both graceful and delicate. A bewitching smile graced his lips.

His eyes, the same dark hue as his hair, narrowed at the elf knelt before him.

"M-my Lord, is it true that...that you can grant me my heart's desire?"

"It is...so long as you are willing to make the pledge. You've heard of it, yes? Sacrifice yourself according to my divine will...and I will see to your future."

As the god replied, he bestowed upon her a smile of the divine, seductive and yet full of blessing.

The elf was entreating him with her gaze, but then, hands shaking, she removed her robe and exposed her bare back to the slender god. He responded by scoring his finger with a knife, releasing droplets of red blood.

She was receiving the god's blessing; his Falna.

Once the hieroglyphs had been carved into her back, she was reborn as a follower of her new god.

"This goes for everyone as well! Once the promised day has arrived, I shall make all your desires reality! All your dreams! Pledge yourself to my name...to Thanatos!!"

The robed figures immediately raised a great shout. Their bodies trembled with fervor, and some had tears running down their faces at the sheer flood of emotion.

"Long live Lord Thanatos!"

"Please...please make our dreams come true!!"

Again and again, his name rang through the hall, reverberating against the rock and stone.

The god, Thanatos, smiled down at them from his altar.

Their cries still ringing in his ears, he turned his back as he made his way out of the hall into the dark passage behind the altar. Soon, the blue glow of magic-stone lanterns surrounded him, with nothing but the echo of his own footsteps accompanying him in the gloom.

He walked until a woman, her back against the passage wall, came into view.

"Nice work today, Lord Thanatooooooos."

She was human, and on her shoulders hung an overcoat of feathers and skins—drop items from monsters in the Dungeon. Beneath it, she wore only close-fitting fabric over her chest and tight leather pants to cover her legs.

The smile she gave him was derisive, at best.

"Seems like you're gettin' the hang of this whole high-and-mighty bit, hmm?"

"Hardly. More like gettin' a crick in the neck! Sure you don't wanna switch with me, Valletta dear?"

The god's captivating aura disintegrated in a flash. The alluring gaze and grin he'd directed toward his followers devolved into the facade masking a god with far too much time on his hands. With that air of dignity gone, all that remained was his degeneracy.

"That's soooo dumb. Why would I? There's no point if it's not a god on the job. You need *majesty* to convince those schmucks their dumb little dreams are gonna come true."

"I know, I know! But still! I could have all the children in the world hanging on my every word and it still wouldn't be enough…And don't deny that officials and leaders in the mortal realm aren't doing the exact same thing. This is gonna get even worse as the organization grows."

The girl, Valletta, stepped away from the wall, sidling over and latching onto Thanatos's back.

"Did you need something, by the way? I'm sure you're not just here to give me a hard time."

"We have a visitor," she responded, pointing her chin farther down the passage to a fluttering swath of red hair, wreathing around a pair of green eyes and a face that was callous and cold.

It was the red-haired woman, neither human nor monster but a "creature."

"Well, hello there, Levis dear. It's been a while. You need something?" Thanatos started toward the woman, ever-present smile on his face.

"I have a message from that masked Ein. 'It's about time for *Loki Familia* to show up.'"

This stopped him in his tracks.

"…I see. Then they're coming after all. What's the plan?"

"Lure them here…and trap them. Kill all of them except Aria."

"Aria…? Ah, the little Sword Princess. What about you, Levis? What will you do?"

"—I will deal with Aria." Levis's voice suddenly intensified with her reply, a strange, disquieting aura surrounding her. Intimidation, perhaps, or was it simply her presence? At any rate, she seemed entirely different from when she previously crossed swords with the girl revered as the Sword Princess. A lust for blood permeated Levis's taut green eyes.

"Wait just a minute here, Levis. I'll do what you ask, but hear me out. Or maybe *help* me out would be the better choice of words. *Loki Familia*'s no joke! Not sure I can do all that on my own."

"I don't care. Figure something out."

"Come on! This is the surface, yeah? Luring them here is all well and good, but if they get a look at those spirits? Won't be pretty."

"..."

As Levis started to turn to leave, Thanatos fearlessly laid a hand on her shoulder.

She batted it away, turning to look him square in the eye. "I will dispose of Aria…That is all I can offer and all you need." Without another word, she walked off, disappearing into the shadow of the passage.

Though Thanatos deflated a little in response to the ever-callous resident of the underground, his features betrayed an inkling of amusement.

"Thanatos. Leave Finn to me. No matter what happens, yeah?" Valletta asked with a venomous smile.

"Right, you have your own bone to pick with him, if I remember correctly. By all means, have your fun." Thanatos nodded in return. "Though I'll be screwed if you *don't* take care of him." A blanket of gloom seemed to settle atop him—until he suddenly remembered something with an "Ah!"

"Why don't we pay our dear Barca a visit, too?"

Clang, clang.

The sound echoed in the darkness of the tunnel.

A man's bloodied hands wielded hammer and pick; nobody knew how long they had toiled. Long bangs hung over his left eye, while under his right was a deep bag, and his skin was so pale it was as if it had completely forgotten the warmth and light of the surface sun.

Like a doll, he tirelessly worked, digging his hole, almost as though the devil himself possessed him.

CHAPTER 1

ORARIO NOW

Гэта казка іншага сям'і

Цяпер лабірынта горада

"Nnnnnggghhhhh…!"

Lefiya was shaking.

As her uncontrollable emotions sent shudders through her body, a wordless, guttural moan tumbled out from her thin lips.

For you see, a *certain piece of news* had made its way to her home, Twilight Manor, setting its residents abuzz.

"That bastard…!!"

"Bete, you big lug! Lemme see!!"

Bete was holding the parchment with the news between tightly clenched fists in the manor's dining hall while Tiona pressed him so she could have a look. A considerable crowd had already gathered around him. Aiz, Tione, Raul, Aki—everyone, from first-tier adventurers to the rookies, couldn't believe their ears when they heard the news.

It had hit the papers that morning.

Before the excitement of a certain "meeting" had a chance to die down, a bit of information was stirring a frenzy of excitement among the adventurers.

—Bell Cranell had reached Level 3.
—In a mere month.

Everything had started a week prior, when *Hestia Familia* and *Apollo Familia* had conducted their War Game—a "proxy war" of sorts meant to settle their dispute. Given the pleasure-seeking antics of the gods and goddesses in Orario, it had turned into a major affair involving the entire city. Then, somehow or another, the underdog, *Hestia Familia*, had come out on top—a feat that had everyone buzzing with stories of slaying giants.

But now this? While Orario was still at fever pitch? It was only natural for the members of *Loki Familia* to be equally as flabbergasted as the rest of the city.

"Aiz, Aiz, Aiz, look, look, look! Little Argonaut! Level Three! Can you believe it?!" Tiona bounded over toward the swordswoman in question, all smiles.

"Yeah, he's...really something else," Aiz responded with a series of thoughtful nods.

"Still, don't you think it's a little bit...weird?" Tione said, as perplexed as everyone else. "Maybe it has something to do with that time he beat the minotaur. When all his abilities maxed out, you know? What do you think, Riveria?"

"It's certainly not a feat achievable by mere effort alone. An undiscovered growth ability perhaps...or a rare skill? With something like that, it's considerably more plausible."

"Hmm, well, I don't think even the most extraordinary of powers would make it easy for him to trounce both the minotaur as well as Phoebus Apollo's Hyacinthus..."

Bete only offered a disgruntled "Hmph!"

Next to the group, the catgirl and human pair, Anakity and Raul, were having a conversation of their own among their fellow second-tier familia members.

"Bell Cranell...Didn't he come to the manor once?"

"Sure did. He said he wanted to see Miss Aiz. Pissed everyone the hell off, too..."

Bell Cranell wasn't exactly a favorite of *Loki Familia*'s lower-level members—for multiple reasons—which made this piece of news particularly unwelcome. None of them wanted to acknowledge this new feat of his, no matter how well he'd stood his ground against opponents that far outranked him.

Needless to say, the latest development in the tale of the Little Rookie was the number one topic of conversation in the dining hall that morning, and it even drew in Finn and the other elites, as well.

"Bet it's all thanks to my and Aiz's help—Whoops! That's a secret! Eh-heh-heh...Still, though. Pretty exciting!"

In an especially animated mood, Tiona gushed to her enthusiastic companions.

Lefiya, on the other hand, could only stand there shaking as she eyed the others.

Just what is going on here?! Does no one think this is bizarre?!

So what if *Hestia Familia* had felled the giant? Big deal!

Well, it certainly was a big deal, but that was a different matter entirely.

It's just as Miss Tione said—his growth is simply too fast! Suspiciously so...! He reached Level 2 only a short while ago!!

That feat had been remarkable enough. Now this!

And *Loki Familia* hadn't even had time to catch their breath upon returning from Port Meren and their scuffle with *Kali Familia*. In the time it had taken them to sleep off their fatigue back in the manor, a conflict had broken out between Hestia and Apollo, the already overzealous gods had stirred the pot—even Loki had joined in—finally culminating in the War Game. To top it all off, the Little Rookie had leveled up.

For Lefiya, she had returned from her trip only to find her rival was suddenly the same level as her. All in all, it seemed much more likely to have occurred in the Dragon Palace of the fairy tales of the Far East than in reality.

It took me two years to reach Level 3...!

The white rabbit was practically on the verge of overtaking her, though she could already hit Level 4 if she wanted. Still, the shock hit her like a two-ton brick to the face.

The War Game report made the rounds from adventurer to adventurer until it reached Lefiya's hands. As she stood there, staring at his portrait, her hands began to tremble, the paper clenched between them threatening to release a crumpled scream.

"Hey, hey! Lefiya! What do you think of Little Argonaut's... erm...?" Tiona started.

"If I felt like it, I could become Level Four anytime I want... I'm not bitter at all! Not one bit...!! No, that is a lie! An infuriating lie! How could I think of saying that at a time like this, when...when in the blink of an eye he could very well...No! I refuse to lose. I refuse...!!"

The sheer demonic energy exuding from Lefiya's every pore as her body shuddered was enough to stop Tiona in her tracks. Everyone in the vicinity quickly backed away, envisioning the great fire that had destroyed the elven forest.

With the flare of animosity, the elven magic user's determination was born anew.

"Is it just me, or is Lefiya kinda terrifying right now?"

"Yes, Lefiya is also...really something else." Aiz nodded at Tiona's comment.

"Well, she's at an age of complicated emotions. We should give her some space."

Riveria seemed to have gotten a sense for how Lefiya was feeling and offered some advice to the others as their elder.

Aiz, in her own way, also had considerable interest in the Little Rookie's recent level-up due to her constant desire to become stronger, but...even her concern paled in the face of Lefiya's current state. Nevertheless, as the boy's face rose to the forefront of her mind, she made a mental note to pay him a visit.

"It's quite lively for this hour of the morning..." Tione muttered. "Captain?"

"What is it, Tione?"

"Do we have plans for what to do next? I know there was the War Game and all, but...we never did find anything on that second entrance to the Dungeon during our investigation of Meren. Where do we go from here?" she asked, glancing at Lefiya, Aiz, and the others.

Loki Familia's recent trek to Meren had been for exactly that reason—to find any information they could on the elusive second entrance to the Dungeon. They'd need to uncover it if they had any hope of putting a stop to the secret maneuvers of both the Evils' Remnants and the Corrupted Spirit.

"Hmm…Well, I'm sure Loki will figure out something for us shortly…" the prum captain concluded, only half believing his own words. "Who knows. Maybe we'll move our investigation to Daedalus Street?"

"So! To no one's surprise, our top contender for Orario's most suspicious spot is Daedalus Street, am I right?" Loki asked, looking out at the faces of her fellow gods. They were occupying their usual high-class pub—in the room with the soundproofing to ensure no prying ears caught wind of their conversation.

"More like there's nowhere else left, I'd say."

"I've been combing the streets the last three weeks together with Dionysus's kid. We turned any place even remotely suspicious inside out, but no cigar, it would seem. Not a single noteworthy find."

After Dionysus spoke from his spot at the round table, Hermes quickly added his own comment.

This was the first time they were meeting since *Loki Familia*'s return from Meren, and the three gods were taking the opportunity to share the new information they'd uncovered after some time without seeing one another. They'd each brought with them their respective escorts to watch over the proceedings: Dionysus had the elf, Filvis; Hermes had Lulune, the chienthrope; and Loki had Gareth.

"We've had the answer in front of us the whole time; we just didn't see it. Think about it: If you wanna hide a tree, stick it in a forest. Likewise, you wanna hide an entrance to the Dungeon? Hide it in a maze…Have we actually found anything there, by the way?"

"On Daedalus Street? Not a thing. And we searched, Loki, trust me. That area is…special, even compared with vast Orario as a whole."

Hermes shrugged, his smile laced with irony as Loki took a glass of wine sitting on the table and downed it like so much water.

It was just as Loki had said herself back when they'd first

formed their unlikely alliance: They already knew their most likely target.

Daedalus Street.

Known as the *Dungeon on the surface*, the area was the brainchild of the master craftsman Daedalus himself.

"That's the only place in the city we've yet to untangle. Considering the general populace is still very much in the dark about this second entrance, Loki's guess may very well be correct...What's more, Daedalus Street is a stone's throw away from the city's eastern side where the Monsterphilia was held."

When Dionysus mentioned the surprise appearance of the violas at the event, Loki nodded.

"Daedalus Street it is, then. Maybe we'll head out there tomorrow and check things out."

"And you're all right with that, Loki?"

"Oh, stop asking me like you weren't gonna have me do it all anyway! I know you." She flashed them a cold stare, which elicited forced chuckles from the two gods in question.

They were so in sync, Loki couldn't help the suspicion forming in her mind as she watched their chummy behavior. She snorted to let them know she thought complaining about it was more trouble than it was worth.

"At any rate, Finn and my kids will have had enough time to rest up by this point...plus we're finally about to get a good look at our enemy,"

It was true—between the various situations they'd dealt with and the clues they'd uncovered, the threads connecting the fragments of the truth were starting to come together. They were on their way to finally ripping the mask off their enemy.

"Time to make 'em pay for thinkin' their harebrained scheme could actually take down Orario," Loki added quietly. The hawkish smile rising to her lips was enough to make Lulune and Filvis flinch. Gareth, on the other hand, merely sighed beside the warmongering god.

Hermes continued unfazed amid the reactions, still wearing his ever-charming smile as he asked, "By the way, whatever became of your Meren investigation, Loki? I've heard tell it became quite the ordeal."

"Oh, that? We made a few finds. Completely unrelated to that ridiculous fight with Kali and her troupe, though."

Loki offered a short explanation before spreading out documents on the round table—they described Njǫrðr's mysterious human contact for his dealings, as well as his accomplice in transporting the violas into the city: *Ishtar Familia.*

"Njǫrðr certainly went to some surprising lengths to protect the peace in the ocean…Quite the bold plan, buying up violas. Where did he come across this human?"

"In the sewers, apparently. No idea if he's got anything to do with our Evils friends, but *somethin'* sure smells fishy," Loki replied, placing on the table the refined portrait Njǫrðr had drawn of the individual in question. One eye was covered by his long bangs, and the other was deeply sunken, making him seem rather suspicious. His doleful expression indicated he was a man with an obsession.

"And then there's Ishtar. Considering what we know of her and where she spends her time, an investigation itself wouldn't necessarily be difficult. However…" Dionysus started, his princely features crinkling.

"Honestly? She's bound to be even harder to feel out than our sewer dweller," Loki agreed. "Though, at least accordin' to Njǫrðr, she's interested in him for her own reasons."

Ishtar Familia was one of Orario's premier familias. Not only did she have her fair share of military might with the Berbera under her command, she also controlled many of the city's brothels—which meant the majority of the Pleasure Quarter. This grip on the Night District made her nigh untouchable from the Guild's perspective. To wrongly confront her would mean turning the Pleasure Quarter and all its supporters against them. Considering how many people worshipped the Goddess of Beauty, there was bound to be considerable backlash from that angle, as well.

Above all, Ishtar was clever, as was already apparent during the

Meren ordeal. Just thinking about her and the disturbances she seemed to be connected to was enough to make Loki wrinkle her nose in frustration.

"Ishtar, huh…?" Hermes suddenly murmured after his long, contemplative silence. "Perfect…Loki, Dionysus, allow me to look into this, would you?"

"Huh?"

The other two gods eyed him suspiciously at his sudden offer.

"What's this all of a sudden, huh? You're usually the one passin' the buck—not takin' it!" Loki balked.

"Oh-ho-ho, I can do my part sometimes, too, you know."

"You do realize you're going up against one of Orario's most distinguished familias, yes? One careless move and you could very well lose your head," Dionysus pointed out.

"Really now, there's no need to be so concerned. I just so happen to be right in the middle of fulfilling a request for Ishtar. Even if I probe a little, it won't seem suspicious at all. And if something did happen…my adorable children would be there to catch my fall!"

"G-gimme a break, Lord Hermes…!"

Hermes answered with a laugh while Lulune groaned with a long-suffering expression and drooping tail, unsure if the deity under her watch was being serious or not.

"Loki has already expressed her displeasure. I'll do my work properly…so leave Ishtar and hers to me," Hermes finished with a soft smile, standing up from the table. Grabbing Lulune, he left the room.

"…A real troublemaker, that one. Does whatever the hell he wants whenever the hell he feels like it. Not sure I'll ever understand why he does what he does," Loki grumbled.

"I'm afraid he's always been like this…" Dionysus responded, nonplussed. He glancing toward the door Hermes had gone through. As his golden hair shifted, he narrowed his glass-like eyes. "And yet I'd watch out for him if I were you, Loki…"

"Huh? Where'd that come from? Kinda late in the game to be saying we can't trust 'im, don'tcha think?"

Dionysus kept his eyes on the door. "I'm sure you've noticed this already, but...we're not the only ones Hermes is cooperating with. He also has Ouranos on his side."

"..."

"I understand that Hermes, too, suffers the pain of having lost a child—a victim, the same as us—so I don't doubt his reasons for cooperating...However, I'm positive that old god is pulling the strings. Giving him too much information and allowing him free rein will only play into Ouranos's plans," Dionysus explained. His distrust and unease toward the Guild's overseer was plain.

"If yer so worried, why'd you invite him here in the first place?"

"I thought he might be of some use...And also, I'm interested in knowing just what Ouranos is hiding," he replied, eyes turning toward the goddess. "Loki, I know you've said he may very well be clean, but even if he doesn't have anything to do with the Corrupted Spirit, he's hiding something else...something bigger...it could very well make Orario fall into chaos. Or, at least, that's how I feel. Which is why I just can't bring myself to trust the Guild...or him," he told her clearly. "I wonder if some calamity doesn't await us in the old god's divine will."

Loki remained quiet, neither agreeing nor dissenting.

"Also...I have reason to believe Hermes may have his own goal, as well. A personal one."

"?"

"Colluding with us, playing lapdog to that old man—everything's part of his own plans. You saw the grin on his face as he left. He's up to something."

That was when Dionysus finally fell silent, almost as though he were about to warn Loki of some unbeknownst Irregular. When they saw the look on his face, both Filvis behind him and Gareth in his spot beside Loki gave him their undivided attention.

"...Which is why all I ask is that you watch out for him. I get the feeling we could be in for some rough waters thanks to him."

"..."

Dionysus let out a tired sigh before bringing his now-cold tea to his lips.

Loki glanced at him before turning her attention to the door, recalling the image of Hermes and the meaningful smile on his lips just before he'd left.

Daedalus Street was an expansive residential quarter located in southeast Orario.

Residential though it may have been, its architectural makeup bordered on the obtuse. Stairs ran the length of the multistoried buildings rising from the stone in all shapes and sizes, and the sheer amount of alleyways or side streets was enough to confuse even the most directionally gifted. It was called the "Dungeon on the Surface," and for good reason—one wrong turn was enough to become forever lost in the neighborhood's mazelike roads, and not just for those unaccustomed to its twists and turns. Even those who'd long lived there had to be careful lest they lose their way.

It had been constructed close to one thousand years prior—almost immediately after the gods had descended from the heavens, apparently—in what was known as the Divine Era. A monument to Orario's past artisans, it was created by the renowned craftsman (and its namesake) Daedalus.

"This place always amazes me…"

"If one were to get lost here, I highly doubt they'd be able to find their way back…"

The sun had just started its ascent from the eastern horizon when *Loki Familia* began their trek to Daedalus Street.

As soon as they entered the labyrinth, Tiona murmured her impression, taking in the sights around her, and Lefiya echoed the sentiment. As Aiz listened to their comments, she found herself mentally nodding in agreement.

If it was possible to disregard the signs of modern life—laundry hanging out on lines, old folks absorbed in their games of chess along the roadside—it was easy to mistake the area for a set of ancient ruins.

"Like I discussed back in the manor, there's a mighty high chance our elusive *quarry* is right here on this very street. Alls we gotta do is find it. I know it's gonna be a pain, but…let's do it!"

Loki exclaimed exuberantly from the front of the group, doing her best to avoid naming the target of their search: a second entrance to the Dungeon. Behind her trailed the women of her familia, Aiz included, and no one else. Finn and the rest of *Loki Familia*'s men were off on a mission of their own.

"Find it, sure. But how? All we have to go off of is this picture!"

"Asking the locals, maybe? After that, not much else we can do but search every single nook and cranny."

Holding the sketch of the man they were targeting, Tione gave a weary groan at Loki's answer.

There likely wasn't an adventurer in all of Orario who'd take on a task like this—searching Daedalus Street for a person who may or may not be there—no matter how much money was involved.

"The Sword Princess…Amazon the Slasher…Jormungand…and is that…Nine Hell, even?! Hot damn!"

"Lai, what gives? Stop pushin'!"

"They're so pretty…and so cool, too."

The appearance of the most famous familia in Orario was enough to draw the awed gazes of the locals, watching from a short distance away. Aiz directed a soft smile toward a trio of children—human, chienthrope, and half-elf—who were staring at her particularly starry-eyed as they walked past.

*I don't come here too often…*she thought, her golden eyes scanning the perimeter. The fashion of the area was very different from what residents of the Main Streets usually favored. More subdued.

Many of the city's underprivileged made Daedalus Street their home. In fact, not even the most downtrodden of familias or adventurers frequented its streets anymore, while more and more it was becoming a nesting ground for rogues and thieves. Though this lack of public order wasn't obvious by looking at the locals, it still required attention. The area certainly made for a perfect place to hide a second entrance to the Dungeon—alongside other plans of nefarious intent.

"I'm startin' to think this place is even more of a labyrinth than the Dungeon itself!"

"I'd ask what you mean by that, but I'm more interested in what you'd have us do next, Loki."

"Guess we can find a meetin' place of sorts, then spread out to look for clues…Huh?"

Loki started to answer Riveria's question before coming to a sudden halt as something caught her eye.

Aiz and the rest of the girls came to a stop, too, following Loki's gaze to where a crowd was beginning to gather nearby. In front of the assemblage, with her back to a fountain in the middle of the square, stood an elderly goddess.

"Bring out your valis, filthy with the prints of covetous fingers! Relieve yourself of the excess of the body and soul! Only when you truly have nothing can the bounties of your hardships be reaped! Only then can your souls be cleansed!" the goddess exclaimed. In one hand, she held a bone wrapped with fresh meat and, in the other, a bottle of wine. Food particles and flecks of her drink decorated her wrinkled lips.

As she held out her arms, the crowd of people cheered in exuberance.

"Hail Lady Penia!"

"Lady Penia! Please accept this wretched pittance I have hoarded for my own selfish desires—a humble offering for your ladyship!"

One after another, impassioned demi-humans brought forth large offerings of valis, presenting them to the goddess. Soon, a sizable pile had formed at her feet, swelling until it was enough to put the musicians and bards who earned their money on the streets to shame.

"What in the…world?" Tiona murmured in bewilderment, voicing the thoughts currently running through the rest of *Loki Familia*'s heads. It was a strange sight to behold.

"You! Gawking at me from the street! You, too, shall offer before me…Oh? Is that Loki I see?"

"So this is where you ended up…is it, Penia?" Loki mused, equally as astonished at the unseemly state of her fellow deity.

The elderly goddess, Penia, could be described in a single word—*squalid*. Clothed in a set of rags that could barely be called a robe, her long white hair hung down in tangles from the top of her head. While her divine nature kept her skin free from stains and dirt, it did little for her dignity, which was nowhere to be found. In fact, she looked altogether like an enchanting witch from the fairy tales of old who had since aged and fallen on hard times—or, at least, that was the first thought that popped into Aiz's mind as she took in the sight of the old goddess.

"Is this goddess a…friend of yours, Loki?"

"*Friend* might be a bit too strong of a word for our relationship…"

Riveria's brows furrowed as she whispered in Loki's direction, unable to believe the person they were examining could be a goddess, and Loki replied somewhat ambiguously.

"I know her…but it ain't like there's a god I don't know, so…" she prefaced before continuing. "She's kind of a joke among us gods. 'Oh no! Here comes Penia the disease! Don't let her touch you!' That kinda thing. But it's true most everyone'd hightail it away as soon as they hear her name. Up in Heaven, she'd go around snatchin' all our savings right out from under our noses…She's like poverty on legs."

The goddess Penia.

Ruler of poverty.

Black sheep of the gods.

"There's no need to be rude, is there? Especially when penury is the one thing that can cleanse both human and god alike! Really now. The only one who doesn't treat me like some babbling old kook is Hestia!"

"Hey, I just call 'em like I see 'em, you eternally destitute panhandler…What are you even doing, anyway?"

"You can't tell? I'm preaching the wonders of poverty to my adorable children!" Penia replied with a broad grin.

Apparently, all the people in the square were her worshippers, hanging on her every word and abiding by her teachings. Some appeared to be merchants of considerable fortune, presenting her generous donations of extraneous money and goods. The sight was less like a proper familia complete with god and followers and more like a new religion.

According to Penia, wealth was nothing but a "corruptor of the soul." Something that would "deprive the body of manual labor." Which, to be fair, made sense. It was a common message and seemed rooted in truth.

The problem was Penia herself, preaching these ideas while feasting greedily on fresh meats until her cheeks bulged. All in all, it smacked of hypocrisy, at least to Aiz and the rest of *Loki Familia*. In their eyes, Penia was nothing more than a goddess taking advantage of her children in order to enjoy an indulgent life in the mortal realm.

"They seem like a familia and yet…they're not…"

"It's not altogether uncommon, though. Gods descending to this world in search of their own salvation, soliciting help from their followers rather than bestowing their blessings…"

"What are you saying, that they're brainwashed?"

"Look at how much money she's made without havin' to lift a finger!"

Aiz, Lefiya, Tione, and Tiona each expressed a mixture of wonder and incredulity as the realization of just what was going on hit home—an accomplishment, for sure, considering the elderly goddess hadn't even formed an actual familia.

However, all was not as it seemed, as apparently Penia gifted most of the offerings she received back to the poor of Daedalus Street as a sort of blessing, which was the one reason she wasn't accused of being a fraud as she made her rounds. The Goddess of Poverty had the support of nearly everyone who lived in the slums.

"The matriarch of the slums…it would seem." Riveria sighed. None of them had ever laid eyes upon such a god. Even the high elf found it a bit too much, never mind how Aiz and the others felt.

Loki, however, just leaned forward curiously.

"Hey, Penia. Just wondering—how long you been down in this dump, huh? A long time, I reckon."

"A long time? To me, it's been nothing more than the blink of an eye, but if you were to ask one of my children, I suppose they would say a few centuries or so."

"Perfect! Then tell me—you ever seen this bloke before?" Loki exclaimed before holding up the detailed portrait of their mysterious gentleman.

Penia's eyes fell toward the man's melancholic face. "...And what business do you have with this human?"

"Need him for a little adventure is all. Wondered if he might hang out on Daedalus Street, so we came to track 'im down," Loki explained, sparing Penia the details as the elderly goddess studied the portrait.

Finally, Penia raised her gaze to Loki and her followers. Then she snorted.

"I've never seen him before in my life. At least, not around here. And even if I did know him, I wouldn't give up information so freely to the likes of you."

"Sooooo...if we paid up, you'd help us?"

"Don't make me laugh! You think I *like* going out of my way for people? I want nothing to do with this!" Penia huffed, turning her back on the group. "No, no, it won't do! My place is right here, with these glittering beauties," she continued as she hefted up the bulk of the offerings from her followers, then vacated the square.

"Guess that's that, then...Was hopin' we'd get at least a little help from the big bosses around here, even if they didn't know anything..."

"Then we'll move forward with just us, as planned?" Riveria asked, to which Loki replied with an agreeing sigh.

Trying to work herself back up, Loki turned toward the rest of the group. "All right, then! Let's get this party started, shall we? We'll split up from here, usin' this square as our meetin' point. Let's say... two groups to start, yeah? Considering how easy it is to get lost here."

"Two groups? You don't think that's a little extreme?" Tione interjected.

"Remember what happened back in Meren with that short pain in the ass? You can't be too careful, I say, 'specially if our enemies know this place like the back of their hand."

When Tione interrupted Loki's orders, the goddess's reply was enough to convince everyone. They didn't want a repeat of what had happened in Meren, after all, when *Kali Familia* had kidnapped Lefiya.

With that decided, they reorganized themselves into two units. Loki and Riveria headed one, comprising mostly lower-level familia members. The other contained, among others, *Loki Familia*'s close-knit quartet: Aiz, Tiona, Tione, and Lefiya.

"But if we just go searching around without any sort of plan, we're totally gonna get lost, right? What now?"

"Hee-hee-hee...Don't worry! I know just what to do."

Tiona seemed discouraged as she gazed out across the convoluted expanse of roads before them, but her sister turned to her with a grin, as if she had something up her sleeve.

"They have those ariadne guides all along the road, right? So long as we follow those, no matter how lost we get, we'll always wind up back at the exit! Even the people who live here use those when they're in a bind. Or at least that's what I've heard."

True to Tione's words, red lines had been drawn on the walls of the square, indicating the direction of the exit. Lefiya and Tiona tilted their heads curiously at the sight.

"Erm, while this is true..."

"What're you tryin' to get at, Tione?"

"Well, if it was me personally trying to pull some kinda nefarious scheme down here, I'd wanna make sure nobody could find it—not just adventurers but even the people who live here. So I'd make my own ariadne guides...leading in the opposite direction of my secret base."

Listening next to her, Aiz let out an "Ah!" of realization. "Then...if we go in the opposite direction of those ariadne guides..."

"Exactly! We should end up smack on our enemy's doorstep!"

"Wow!" Tiona and Lefiya shouted in unison. An eager murmur ran through the rest of the party, too, as they realized there could be some merit to the suggestion.

"I've got a good feelin' about this now!"

"Yes, the theory was certainly persuasive..."

"What else did you expect? The captain's left the capture of this criminal in the capable hands of yours truly, after all!" Tione boasted, crossing her arms across the sizable curves of her chest after Tiona and Aiz offered their approval.

The desire to avoid letting down the man she loved so passionately had produced a rare perceptiveness in the Amazon, though to Lefiya, at least, it was evidence that the true genius lay in whatever it was Finn had told her.

"Anyway, so long as there's no objections, let's get going!"

With the square and Riveria's group at their backs, Aiz's group set off with a triumphant Tione taking the lead as they made their way into the twists and turns of Daedalus's maze.

However.

"We haven't found a single damn thing!" Tiona's exasperated cry echoed through Daedalus Street *at night* as she waved her hands in dismay. "Never mind discovering the enemy hideout, we're too busy being hopelessly lost!! What're we supposed to do *now*, Tione, huh? Look how dark it is!"

"Would you just shut up for a second?! This...this wasn't supposed to happen, okay?! This wasn't...supposed to..."

As the two sisters quibbled, the rest of the group had taken to leaning wearily along the nearby walls, worn near to their cores. The exception was Aiz, currently fretting nervously off by herself.

It was already the middle of the night. The sun's light had long since vanished. As it turned out, the name "Dungeon on the Surface" was no overstatement, given how its twisting streets had completely decimated Tione's naive plan of attack. The more their group had ignored the ariadne guides, the deeper in they ended up, repeatedly encountering dead ends or going around in circles through the same passageways.

"I thought I understood…but Daedalus Street is truly a struggle…" Lefiya muttered, feeling beyond exhausted, and Aiz couldn't help but nod in agreement.

Even when they tried sticking to exactly one of Daedalus's roads, they soon found it splitting into countless smaller byways, almost like a convoluted web. The number of stairs and hills they'd climbed and descended made it feel as though they were trapped in a never-ending spiral. Strange buildings towered above them on either side, like a set of opposing cliff faces connected with a network of crisscrossing stone as intricate as the passages below. The sight of all that blackened brick on top of the weaving roads was enough to make their heads spin, looking more like an optical illusion than an actual place. Leene, the healer and support member of their group, had made a heroic attempt to map out the roads as they'd walked, but halfway through she simply gave up, frustrated tears welling in her eyes as she'd exclaimed, "This is impossible!"

Daedalus Street had oft been described as a window into the depraved mind of an eccentric lunatic. More and more, they were beginning to see why. Even Aiz, at home as she was in the winding corridors of the Dungeon, was having trouble keeping her head straight in this residential labyrinth.

"So, um…what should we do…? Perhaps, we could…head back to the square?"

"No way! I have to at least bring something back. What'll the captain think of me otherwise?!"

"We could be here for days and we still wouldn't find anything!"

Aiz made a tentative suggestion, but Tione insisted while her sister wearily tried to object. With the party's opinion divided, they were at an impasse.

"Lefiya!"

"Huh…? Oh, Miss Filvis!"

A lone elf jumped down from a nearby rooftop. Lefiya started as the other first-tier adventurers readied themselves for an attack. They lowered their guard, however, upon realizing the newcomer was Lefiya's acquaintance.

Her jet-black hair swept past crimson eyes as the elf landed, donned in her usual snow-white battle clothes. Thanks to her clothes and demeanor, *Dionysus Familia*'s Filvis was the very image of a shrine maiden.

"What are you doing here?" Lefiya inquired.

"On Lord Dionysus's orders, I've been instructed to cooperate with *Loki Familia*. I realize this may seem sudden, but…will you allow me to join you?"

"O-of course I would! I'd be happy to! Thank you so much!" Lefiya asserted with a warm smile.

Lefiya wasn't the only one who had a history with the dark-haired elf. Aiz had fought beside her during the battle in the twenty-fourth-floor pantry. Tiona's yelling earlier must have cued her in to the party's location.

"Erm…Miss Tione? Would it be all right if Miss Filvis worked with us?" Lefiya turned to Tione this time, barely able to contain her delight.

"Well, more hands on deck couldn't hurt… I guess it's fine?" Tione shrugged, glancing at the rest of the group to receive their nods of approval. Aiz agreed right away, of course, but even the other girls seemed fine with this newest addition.

"Ho-ho, that's great! The more the merrier! Filvis, was it? I'm Tiona! Welcome aboard!" Tiona, all smiles, quickly jumped at the chance to introduce herself, but—

"…Filvis Challia."

—was all she received in return; the earlier warmth the elf had directed at Lefiya was all but gone. The reserved, almost cold response bewildered Tione and the others. Aiz and Tiona, especially, could only blink in silence.

"Ha-ha…ha-ha-ha…" Lefiya laughed awkwardly.

"…Psst. Lefiya, is that elf just super–socially awkward or what?"

"Erm, it's more like, well…she has her reasons…"

"The poor girl! Since we're a party now, let's get along!"

After Tione waved her over, Lefiya did her best to explain. Meanwhile, Tiona called out with her usual cheer but that was soon cut short.

"I may have said that we would be cooperating, but I have no intention of befriending you. It would be improper for all of you to fraternize with a member of another familia as well, no?" Filvis snapped, abruptly turning away.

Her modest clothing, hiding the better part of her surprisingly white skin, made it plain how concerned her people were with propriety, and her behavior was the complete opposite of that of the Amazons, Tiona and Tione. Though her response wasn't necessarily cruel, it was certainly blunt to the point of hostility.

Needless to say, she earned a great many frowns from the members of her new party. This unknown, fussy elf was just too hard to approach.

Somewhat self-consciously, Aiz marveled at being around someone who was apparently even worse with words than she was…but if Lefiya seemed so comfortable around her, she couldn't be that bad, could she?

"What are you and the others doing now, Lefiya?" Filvis asked.

"Erm, well…We were in the middle of an investigation of sorts, but just now we were thinking it might be better to return to our meeting point and regroup with the others…" Lefiya explained, pacing restlessly back and forth between her colleagues and the other elf. She knew all too well the story behind Filvis's alias, Banshee.

For the time being, at least, they decided to head back. She, Filvis, Aiz, and the rest of the group began making their way down the road—following the ariadne guides they'd previously been ignoring—progressing as one big group. A strange silence settled over them; they were all overly conscious of Filvis, who'd fallen in step beside Lefiya.

As Aiz was beginning to lament her own inability to help despite her best intentions—as Lefiya flitted this way and that in awkward confusion—it happened.

"Grrrrr, I can't take it anymore! Will someone just say something already?!" The naive Amazon, notoriously bad at reading the atmosphere, abruptly broke the silence. "C'mon, Leene! You've gotta know somethin' we girls can talk about, yeah? Somethin' real juicy!"

"M-me?! I, erm…you mean like…gossip about our love lives or something?"

The healer's face flushed a brilliant shade of red.

"Yeah! Romance it is, then!" Tiona responded with a full-faced grin of approval.

And then:

"Hey, Filvis! You got anyone you liiiiiiiiiike?"

"Bwuh?!" Filvis almost choked. In less than an instant, her snow-white skin went completely red.

Supportive *oohs* and *aahs* erupted from the other adventurers at the surprise attack from *Loki Familia*'s celebrated vanguard warrior. Lefiya, in particular, was taken aback by Filvis's extreme reaction.

"D-don't you think that information is a bit private to be sharing upon one's first meeting, Amazon?!" Filvis sputtered.

"Oh, c'mon! Gossip is the world's best icebreaker!" Tiona insisted, her smile never faltering.

The sight of her fellow elf in such a panic gave Lefiya shivers.

M-Miss Tiona is…truly amazing! Here I've been trying so long to accomplish what she did in a matter of moments…

Lefiya was forced to recall a moment from some two months ago, when she, Filvis, and Bete had formed a party on their way to the twenty-fourth-floor pantry. Her eyes sparkled with awe and respect for the Amazon and her ability to smash through her opponent's walls without even trying.

"I—I will gossip, too! Erm…Oh! Could it be…your constant companion—Lord Dionysus?!"

"*Lefiya!!*"

"Wow! Crushin' on a god, huh?"

"Though isn't that uncommon, is it? Especially in the more upstanding familias."

Lefiya wasn't about to let this opportunity pass her by, but her "assistance" did little more than turn Filvis's face an even deeper shade of red. Tiona and Tione were more or less unfazed, but the damage had already been done. Soon, the entire group of girls had joined in the conversation, all of them gushing with their own stories of kiss-and-tell.

The only one not participating, in fact, was Aiz, altogether quite unsure what to do with herself given the current topic.

"What about you lot?! If you're going to ask someone, then at least offer something first?!" Filvis demanded.

"I'm after the captain!"

"Me? I'm not really interested in all that lovey-dovey stuff, y'know? But I am rootin' for a certain little adventurer, hee-hee-hee!"

"Did I mention the captain was mine?!"

"I don't really…have anyone in particular, either…though there is someone I look up to…"

"I've got dibs on the captain!!"

"Oh, shut up already, Tione!!" Tiona finally shouted once the other Amazon began to sound like a broken record. Meanwhile, Lefiya could only throw hesitant glances in Aiz's direction upon revealing her heart's weakness.

"What about you, huh, Aki? You and Raul sure hang out a lot."

"Not a chance."

"If it has to be someone in the familia…can't really think of anyone besides the captain."

"Right? It's so unfair how cute and cool he is! I'd like to give him a nice big hug if I could! *Drool*…"

"Tione, puuuut that fist down."

It didn't take long for the entire group to offer up their own thoughts on the matter, and soon the air was buzzing with the distinctive energy of girl talk. Even as they continued noisily down the dark road, it was obvious the familia's prum captain had most of the votes.

"What about you, Leene?"

"Me? Erm…"

Tiona had finally turned to the human girl who'd started the conversation in the first place.

The bespectacled girl played bashfully with the rim of her glasses, braided hair swaying. "…Mister Bete, I suppose."

"Seriously?! You've gotta be kidding!"

"Talk about bad taste, Leene! Bete? Really? The guy going on and on about how 'concerning himself with weaklings is a waste of time' on the last expedition?"

The Amazon sisters balked, unable to believe their ears.

Meanwhile, Leene practically curled in on herself in embarrassment, cheeks aflame.

"Yeah, but…he can be quite gallant when he wants to be…a-and I think he's a good person…deep down…"

"Nahhh, no way! No freakin' way!"

Leene's expression softened as she spoke but Tiona, who was constantly on bad terms with the werewolf, fiercely voiced her doubts.

As Lefiya and the rest of the girls smiled weakly, however, the attention finally turned to the only victim left: a certain golden-haired, golden-eyed swordswoman.

"Right, then. What about you, Aiz?"

"…I don't really…have anyone…"

"Oh, c'mon! You've gotta have at least someone! Even the teensiest bit of a crush!" Tiona continued, urging her on with a smile.

"I…" Aiz struggled to find her words as everyone in the group became intently focused on the Sword Princess's plight—Lefiya in particular. The zealous conversation had originally been intended as a method of inducting Filvis, who was now utterly exhausted, but it couldn't be stopped anymore. Its original purpose had long been forgotten, and the topic was simply too mouthwatering for a group of girls in their prime to resist.

"Aaaaaaaa*choo*!!"

Bete let out a ferocious sneeze, drawing the attention of his peers.

"Caught a cold, have you, Bete?"

"C'mon, Finn, as if! More like some punk somewhere's bad-mouthin' me."

"Come to mention it, you've been shivering a bit yourself, there, Cap'n."

"It is a bit strange. It's just a chill, but it never seems to end."

"Likely Tione and her lot are up to no good again…"

As Finn, Bete, Raul, and Gareth conversed, their voices echoed off the walls of the tunnel surrounding them.

They were in the sewers beneath Orario. While Loki had taken the ladies of the familia to search Daedalus Street, Finn and the rest of the men had been tasked with investigating the winding passages beneath the city.

Among them were ten or so lower-level familia members, each one—including Raul—carrying a portable magic-stone lantern.

"While it may be true that Njǫrðr first met our mysterious gentleman here beneath the city…'twas nigh five years ago now, no? Probably nothing left to find," Gareth mused somewhat despondently.

"I don't disagree with you," Finn replied. "Bete and Loki have both done their share of searching down here, and even the girls and I did our own investigation of the place back when Aiz and the others got caught up in that pantry debacle on the twenty-fourth floor. Though we did find a few violas, there wasn't much else."

"So why are we here now, huh?"

"Because looking for people isn't the same as looking for monsters. Also…we'll be focusing mainly on the section of sewers beneath Daedalus Street—the city's southeastern quarter and its vicinity. If we can at least limit the range of our search, we may just be able to find something."

Finn answered Bete's doubts with no sign of hesitation in his voice.

Equipped with his long spear, the prum captain kept careful watch of their surroundings from his spot in the middle of the group. Likewise, the others readied their weapons lest an unexpected attack catch them off guard. When their superior perception and awareness were focused, even the slightest movement was unable to escape their gazes as they investigated the city's complex sewer system.

Down the dank tunnel they advanced, ears honed toward the sound of flowing water.

"!"

"What's wrong, Bete?"

The werewolf had come to an abrupt stop the moment his foot crossed the threshold between south and southeast—Daedalus Street's border. And he wasn't the only one, either; every animal person present was responding to a certain scent in the air, their noses upturned and sniffing.

"I could recognize this stink anywhere—violas."

Finn's features hardened in an instant. Quickly reorganizing the rest of the group, he herded them forward in a new direction with Bete in the lead. The werewolf's metal boots were pointed directly toward the Old Sewerway. Passing through the antiquated double-swinging iron gate, they crossed over a stone bridge, the intervals between their echoing footsteps urging them to hurry.

Finally...

"...A hidden staircase?"

It was in a small passage jutting off from the main waterway. The opening leading downward was just slightly ajar, almost as if its "lid" had slipped, the panel of stone wide enough that even the long bodies of the violas would probably have had no problem passing through.

"We found a whole lot of nothing last time...and now this just appears. Seems pretty fishy, if you ask me..." Bete muttered under his breath, and anxiety gripped the rest of the group as they grasped the implications.

It was enough to make Finn and Gareth narrow their eyes suspiciously, but they ordered the group to proceed down the stairs all the same. The make of this new stone tunnel was considerably different from that of the sewers up above, and the residual scent of monsters permeated the air around them Still, they continued—until they stumbled upon something.

"A gold...door?" Raul murmured in awe.

"That shine...It's orichalcum!" Gareth was equally as astonished.

The brilliant golden door standing before them now was well over three meders tall.

Within the flawless silvery luster, the glitter of red gemstones could be seen.

The men of *Loki Familia* could only look upon the soaring structure in wonder, unable to speak.

CHAPTER
2

DUNGEON
TRAP

Гэта казка іншага сям'і.

Dungeon пастка

Ka-chunk. Ka-chunk.

The sound of dirt being carved away echoed throughout the darkness.

First came the swing of a hammer, followed by the pounding of a nail. Again and again, for long hours, the work continued in that dark tunnel.

"You don't suppose you could help us with a little something, do you, Barca dear?"

"...Leave me be, Thanatos."

The light from Thanatos's lantern flickered off the shadowy walls as he stood behind the busily digging figure to accost him. The man in question—a human named Barca—neither turned around nor halted in his work. A dark bag sagged beneath the one eye not hidden by his long bangs, making him a dead ringer for the man Aiz and the others were currently hunting.

"There's no time. Even talking to you now is costing me precious moments...You must understand our suffering. The plight of those not blessed with eternal life. Our *masterpiece* is not yet complete..."

"Yes, well, it would seem *Loki Familia* is finally on their way here..."

Though Barca had complained, his soft voice so lifeless one might think he was dead, his hand stilled instantly.

Thanatos watched him for a moment, a smile playing across his lips, before continuing. "They're trouble enough with their constant sniffing around, but if we don't do something about them now, it may make fund-raising more difficult...perhaps. My thoughts were to invite them down here for a bit and have the darkness simply... swallow them up," the god explained to the silent back of his companion. "After all, with them in the way, you wouldn't be able to finish your ancestor's dear labyrinth, now, would you?"

Barca's hands fell limply away from the wall. Finally turning around, ever so slowly, he focused his dark eyes on Thanatos.

"What would you have me do…?"

"There was a certain gadget I thought about using, but…my, my, only you and your ilk are able to control it, yes? Or at least that's what I heard a short while ago."

"…You aim to use our masterpiece to inflict harm, Thanatos?"

"You say that as if we wouldn't lose everything if they were to round us up all at once! Besides, isn't this sort of purpose the exact reason you prepared it in the first place? Or am I wrong?"

"…"

"There's a good boy. I'm counting on you, now."

Thanatos finished talking, his eyes crinkling in mirth.

Barca averted his gaze. "…Let me know when you need me," he finally agreed, nodding with a begrudging jerk of his head.

And then he was back to work. Thanatos let out a chuckle (*"Still stubborn as ever"*) and turned on his heels, leaving his follower behind.

Finn and his group had discovered a door within the city's sewers.

The news was relayed to Aiz and the other women of the fruitless Daedalus Street investigation upon their return to *Loki Familia*'s home, and it was decided they would concentrate their efforts on the new lead.

The next morning, the members of *Loki Familia* (goddess included) gathered in the secret passage leading down to the door in question.

"Damn! So this is that orichalcum door, huh? It's huge!"

"Yeah, and if there's such a wacky-lookin' door here, it's gotta mean we hit the jackpot, right? Their top-secret base."

Tiona reacted with awe, balancing her Urga on her shoulder as she gazed up at the monstrous slab of metal, and Loki sounded completely certain as she murmured to herself.

Just like my Desperate... Aiz thought, and one hand went instinctively to the trusted sword hanging at her waist as she eyed the door from among her circle of peers.

Orichalcum.

The master ingot, integral in the creation of the Durandal from which Superior-grade weapons, like Aiz's Desperate, were forged, stronger even than the adamantite mined in the Dungeon, and easily the highest-grade material in the entire world. It was said that the ingot's method of manufacture, similar to that of mythril, was first established back during the Ancient Times when monsters encroaching on the surface forced all the various races to unite. Long, long ago, before smithing abilities and the blessing of the gods.

Orichalcum was a crystallization of that bygone era as well as the limitless potential of the mortal realm—their wisdom, imbued with the techniques of humans and demi-humans alike.

Making even a dent in this door of orichalcum would be impossible.

Loki was right: If someone had erected a door like this, something must be on the other side. At long last, they'd found their enemy's hideout.

"Even comparing this with the map, there's no question about it: This secret passage must connect with Daedalus Street. It's exactly as Loki predicted."

"And to think it was Bete and those other lunkheads who found it first! Well, I'm less upset about the captain and Gareth, but...Anyway, it feels like a kick in the butt..."

Indeed, the small, hidden passage veering off from their current spot in the Old Sewerway seemed to perfectly line up with the city's third district, sandwiched neatly between the eastern and southeastern main streets. Riveria could clearly see the link to the labyrinthine district, but next to her, Tione let out a despondent groan.

Certainly, the familia's women were ashamed after spending the previous night combing Daedalus Street only to come up empty-handed, though *Loki Familia*'s men didn't share the same feeling.

"There's no reason to feel bad. We only discovered this by chance, almost as if we were lured here on purpose."

"Aye, the old hole was already open and waitin' for us. It was practically askin' us to find it! The reek of monster scum was a bonus."

The girls threw glances at Finn and Gareth.

The others gazed with tense expressions at the door in question.

"Then...you think it's a trap?" Lefiya croaked, her voice echoing off the surrounding stone.

Almost as if affirming her suspicions, the door gave a sudden creak before sliding open.

"!!"

Slowly, slowly, the orichalcum door rolled upward into the rock.

Aiz and the others watched in bewildered shock as the way before them was opened to the dense blackness of the passage beyond. Magic-stone lanterns illuminated the path with blue light, trembling like will-o'-the-wisps in the shadow.

"Finn..." Gareth whispered.

"Yes, I saw it, too," Finn replied, his eyes narrowing. "It's our masked friend...no doubt about it. The one who opened the door is that 'creature.'"

The instant before the door had opened, Finn's green eyes had caught a trace of a figure just before it had disappeared into the darkness—a bluish-purple robe and bizarrely patterned mask. He knew them all too well from the fights they'd had with the creature down in the twenty-fourth-floor pantry and during their expedition to the fifty-third floor.

Their enemy was welcoming them.

"Whew, you saw all that in an instant? Man, you've got good eyes! I didn't see nothin'!" Loki exclaimed, one hand shielding her eyes as she frowned.

"Our senses were amplified thanks to your blessing, after all. Don't group us together with the rest of the common folk. Besides, prums are already known for their sense of perception even among us demi-humans," Riveria countered with exasperation.

Next to her, the prum in question began issuing orders. "Bete. Cruz. Scout out the path up ahead but don't go too far. I want you back here ASAP," he instructed the first-tier and second-tier adventurers. Heeding his urge for caution, the Level-6 werewolf and Level-4 chienthrope darted off noiselessly down the dark hallway.

They returned minutes later.

"Nothing in the direct vicinity of the entrance, sir. No people, no monsters—not a soul! However, the tunnel quickly branches off in multiple directions, almost like a maze...or, I suppose, like the Dungeon."

The normally reticent Cruz relayed their findings in place of Bete.

Hearing him, everyone there imagined soldiers besieging a fortress.

As Finn quieted in thought, the rest of the members behind him began exchanging thoughts of their own.

"Wh-what do you...think we should do, huh?"

"We saved time tryin' to get that door open, didn't we? Let's check it out!"

"But it's gotta be a trap, right?"

"No harm in accepting an invitation, if you ask me. We'll just plow our way through any traps we find!"

"Certainly, we'd be remiss to just stand here twiddling our thumbs after coming all this way..."

At Raul's question, Tiona, Aki, Tione, and the elven Alicia all offered their own opinions.

Riveria turned to the group. "Realistically speaking, we have no choice but to move forward. Considering our enemy's goal is to summon the demi-spirit aboveground, we have to move quickly. If even one of those things was to appear on the surface, Orario would quickly become a sea of fire."

The high elf's words rang true.

Even Finn, his arms folded across his chest as he brooded, found himself nodding in agreement.

They could either take the enemy head-on now or bide their time until the demi-spirit made its way to the surface. The choice was clear.

Loki Familia would give chase now, no question about it. Even if this was a trap, delaying their attack would only make matters worse.

And yet...my thumb is throbbing something awful, Finn thought, dropping his gaze toward his right hand. The digit was sending up tiny pinpricks of pain—a warning of what was to come. It was not dissimilar to the stinging sensation that developed whenever they made their way into the Dungeon's lower depths.

With the silent pressure from Raul, Riveria, and the others weighing on him, he glanced at Loki next to him.

"Yeah, I know...I've got a reeeal bad feelin' about this, too. But it does seem like we don't have much of a choice," Loki admitted, confirming that she, too, had sensed the air of foreboding.

Finn knew his intuition was correct, and he was already running through battle formations in the back of his mind.

Until.

"Finn. Let's leave the dead weight behind, yeah?" Bete implored, breaking his silence as he stared long and hard into the darkness behind the open door. His wolf ears were standing straight up on his head, and his nose twitched several times. "Something stinks. We're not gonna want anything holdin' us back...Get my drift?"

A sullen mood descended over the lower-level members of the group at his callous comment. Tiona and Tione shot him a set of identical glares.

"Hey! We're a familia, aren't we? And familias stick together! So put a cork in it, will ya?"

"Yeah, and just how far do you expect to get without the help of our supporters, huh? This is just like any other time we've headed into the Dungeon. I don't wanna hear you complaining when all our weapons and items are gone!"

Bete answered their defense with a muttered curse. Tiona's response was typical of her, but Tione's point carried considerable weight. After all, if there really was a second entrance to the Dungeon lurking up ahead, they'd need all the numbers they could get.

Gareth let out a sigh as he watched his strong-willed fledglings bicker among themselves. Next to him, Finn reached a decision.

"We'll form up with a front line and a back line, as well as a healing unit. Gareth and I will lead the attack. Riveria will remain here in case of an emergency. Loki and the others will also wait until we know more about the path ahead."

"Understood."

Everyone moved immediately to their tasks once Finn had finished giving his orders. The supporters collected all the spare weapons and items they'd brought with them from the manor. Lefiya had been included in the names Finn listed for the advance party, and she got to work readying her cylindrical backpack with all its equipment. She was in the middle of this task when she heard someone call her name.

"Lefiya...You're...going, too?"

"Miss Filvis...?"

The other elf was still with them after joining the group the night prior. Her crimson eyes were focused directly on Lefiya.

"While I hate to side with that werewolf...I feel it, too. Something's not right. If something were to...happen..." Filvis's eyes remained fixated on Lefiya, though her words were vague.

Lefiya couldn't help the twinge of happiness at the elf's concern, but she responded concisely all the same. "Yes, I will go. I want to protect everyone...Miss Aiz, too."

She was a magic user, after all.

"...I see." Filvis closed her eyes for a moment before bringing a hand to her chest and meeting the eyes of the other elf with a staff in her hands. "Then I shall go, too. To protect you."

She sounded so much like a knight making a vow that Lefiya found herself at a loss for words as a flush of pink rose to her cheeks. Quickly recovering, she smiled and offered Filvis a word of thanks.

They stayed there briefly, two elves sharing a moment of warmth, while the rest of the group bustled about them in their preparations.

"Oh-ho-ho! Whadda we have here, huh? A forbidden elven romance?! What a treat! This is a good time!"

"Exactly what is a 'good time'? Good grief..."

As Loki snickered, ogling the two elves from off to the side, Gareth let out a sigh.

"That all right? Gettin' so close with an elf from another familia?"

"Eh, she did help us out down on the twenty-fourth floor. 'Sides, I may have ever so slightly interrogated her earlier, and it seems like she's actually workin' on her own. The smug little bastard Dionysus has nothin' to do with it," Loki replied.

"That so?"

I want to protect Lefiya.

Earlier, under the all-seeing eyes of the goddess, Filvis had confessed everything.

"She's definitely not lyin'. Lefiya's found herself a real knight in shining armor." Loki tittered.

"...I'll never get used to it, I suppose, try as I might. Elves are far too intense! Gives a dwarf like me the willies," Gareth said, crinkling his eyes and pretending to rub his arms. They watched as the two young elves continued their preparations for the upcoming raid.

"..."

Aiz's ears caught the conversation between goddess and dwarf, causing her to glance at the two elves in question, a smile forming on her face.

It didn't last, however, as the expression faded, and she turned around. Surrounded by the harried activity of her peers, she stared long and hard down the yawning corridor leading to their enemy's hideout.

The party that forged its way into the sewers' depths comprised the first-tier adventurers except Riveria, Raul and the rest of the Level-4 second tiers, and the remaining lower-level members, mostly Level 3s. As a last-minute addition, Filvis also tagged along. They plunged through the darkness of the surrounding stone, Gareth and Tiona in the lead.

"Man, I thought we were going into an enemy hideout...Practically feels like the Dungeon in here!" Tione cursed under her breath.

"Yes," Lefiya agreed. "Admittedly, any sort of stronghold would likely go to great lengths to hinder enemy infiltration...though perhaps this is going above and beyond."

Almost immediately past the door, the passage split into a multitude of dizzying directions. From forks to four-way crossings, the possible paths were nigh uncountable. It seemed with every passing glance, their numbers grew further still, and the adventurers had no choice but to split up and plow their way through.

While the general makeup of the underground maze was typical enough for a labyrinth, its sheer complexity put even Daedalus Street above it to shame. Their only course of action was to send one or two people to scout ahead at each fork, wait for a report on which paths were dead ends, then scour the remaining passageways until they found the proper path.

The tunnels themselves were wide enough for three dwarves to pass comfortably. And they were so uniform in their construction it seemed almost planned, not liable to come crashing down anytime soon. As for the rocks themselves, they appeared considerably aged, many sporting their fair share of cracks and splits. In fact, it almost seemed as though the maze had been built smack in the middle of a set of ancient ruins.

"You know—Whuuuaah?!"

"What's wrong, Raul?!"

"Ah, sorry, it was...nothing. Just a statue. Sorry about that..." Raul recovered from his sudden scream with a forced laugh.

Sure enough, flickering in the light of his portable magic-stone lantern was a demon-like statue that had been placed in the middle of the passage. Aki and the other adventurers who had readied for combat made noises of disapproval.

They had seen similar statues situated every so often along the passageway, in addition to reliefs carved into the stone walls. Though they may have been reluctant to admit it, these fake "monsters" quickly filled their heads with mental images of their very real cousins—namely, the violas.

The bluish glow from the magic-stone lanterns in the walls illuminated the tension in their faces, and their footsteps, normally the last thing on any of their minds, began to feel especially loud. The echoing *clack-clack-clack* of their feet on the stone passageways, impossible to ignore, made their very ears tremble.

"Is it just me, or…does it somehow feel even colder in here than the actual Dungeon?" The uneasy murmur came from Leene, one of the healers who'd been brought along for support.

The Dungeon was "alive," after all—a fact that was common knowledge. The prevalence of Irregulars that so often assaulted them (much to their chagrin) felt more like the abuse of a single living organism than anything else.

This man-made labyrinth, however, was different. They couldn't feel it "breathe."

And this undeniable disparity felt like something inhospitable wrapping itself around them.

Yes…an ever-so-slight chill.

An unsettling quietude. A heavy sense of gloom and obscurity weighing down on top of them.

This wordless, man-made stone labyrinth was slowly enveloping them in inexplicable claustrophobia and hopelessness.

"I know the Unknown Frontier was like this, too, but…I always feel a little anxious in places that haven't been fully mapped out. What happens if we get lost, huh? Can't find our way out. Don't even know which way to go." Tiona was trying to keep the stilted conversation going in an attempt to assuage the worry plaguing the group.

"It's true. Finding yourself in such a situation in the Dungeon would be almost certain death…" Aiz agreed.

"Caves in the mountains were rife with drafts so it was easy to use 'em as guideposts," Gareth added.

They were already deep in enemy territory by this point. Every one of them was braced for a trap.

"What do you mean by that, Gareth?" Tiona questioned as she puzzled over one passage after another.

"The temperature difference 'tween inside an' out can create cave breezes...or so I understand. Think of it like all the air gettin' sucked out the door." Gareth doubled back on himself, expounding on what he knew of mountain caves. "Basically, ye either follow the wind or run counter to it. That's how to avoid winding up at a dead end. Although, the wind often says to squeeze through a hole too small for a man."

"Huh, interesting!"

"You know, you coulda figured that out for yourself if you'd just used that brain of yours for half a second..."

Tiona let out a laugh as she figured it out, while Tione muttered next to her.

Suddenly, Gareth jerked his gaze away to scan the perimeter.

"...Seems the way's shut," he pointed out as his eyes spotted another orichalcum door now blocking their way.

His observation was quickly confirmed, too, as multiple scouts came back with word that all their other paths were similarly blockaded.

"What, are we trapped, then? Should be fine, though. We can always just break through a wall, right?" Tiona boasted, never one to be deterred.

Gareth, however, didn't look so optimistic. "I'm afraid it's not so simple, lass," he countered, and Tiona's eyes widened in puzzlement.

"Huh? Why not?"

The dwarven soldier responded by slamming his fist into the nearest wall. The abrupt cracking sound that resulted was enough to make Lefiya's and Leene's shoulders jump.

"No way...Don't tell me that's...adamantite?!"

"The very same. Covered in a layer of rock, for sure, but underneath, nothin' but rare metal. The whole maze is carved from the stuff! The likes o' you an' me would barely leave a scratch...which means that option's right out."

Tiona's eyes widened further at the sight of all that steely gray beneath the cracked stone.

Adamantite was only a step below orichalcum in terms of strength. Cracking through the who-knows-how-thick wall would be difficult, to say the least, and even if they could make a dent, carving out a hole wide enough for all of them to pass through would take time they didn't have.

The group could do nothing but stare in shock at the news that they were going up against not only doors of orichalcum but a labyrinth made entirely of adamantite.

"You realize the money this ridiculous place musta taken to build? What, did these asshats make a killin' in Meren or somethin'? This is crazy!" Bete exclaimed angrily, echoing the thoughts of the rest of the group.

Neither orichalcum nor adamantite was exactly easy to procure. Collecting this much of both would require labor and funds the likes of which *Loki Familia* could only dream of.

"Certainly not something done in a few years. A decade, maybe? No, probably more...At any rate, the Evils have certainly been busy with some extraordinary projects. In any event, we'd do well not to underestimate them," Finn mused candidly before instructing Raul and the others to demarcate the walls of the paths they'd come by with white chalk.

While keeping an eye on the work of the shrewd adventurer, Aiz began thinking.

Orichalcum doors...Adamantite walls...Breaking in and breaking out are both going to be hard.

The fortress in front of them was virtually impregnable.

This thought alone was disconcerting enough, but there was something else, too—a strange malaise she couldn't quite shake.

What was the point in building such a convoluted maze? Whose idea was it? And this eerie, unsettling sensation from the walls...the feeling of darkness radiating from the maze's very structure...what was it?

—Was this really constructed merely to protect their enemy's hideout?

It was a question she couldn't answer, but setting aside her suspicions for now, she instead turned her attention back to the task at hand—their progress.

Something had finally changed in the corridors.

"There's a staircase up ahead. Seems it goes farther down."

"Same in the opposite direction. No sign of any enemies, either."

—Cruz and Aki returned from their recon duty with the same information. Currently, the group was situated at a T-shaped intersection.

"Plans, Finn?" Gareth asked the prum captain.

"...We'll split into two groups. No matter the direction we choose, fighting is going to be difficult with such a large party if we come under attack," Finn replied before acting on his words and dividing the group in two.

Gareth, Aiz, Tiona, and Tione would be going down the right path.

Meanwhile, Finn himself, along with Bete, Lefiya, and Filvis, would take the left.

Gareth's party would have the greater number of first-tier adventurers in order to balance out the lower-level support members. Naturally, Tione complained about the makeup of the two parties, but the target of her affections himself ultimately persuaded her. Thus, the final two parties, healers included, were evenly split in terms of combat power.

"I'm counting on you, Gareth."

"Aye...Finn?"

"?"

"Don't let 'em get the jump on ya, eh?" Gareth offered amiably.

"...Duly noted. I'll be on my guard," Finn responded with a smile of his own.

Then the two parties broke away, each traveling down their respective path.

"As strange as this is to say...the fact that nothing's attacking us is only making this place feel even creepier..." Raul muttered as he looked around to take in their environs.

"The whole place still reeks of those flowers, though...No question that the ones in the sewer were definitely carried through here." Bete scowled.

The two of them were both part of Finn's group. The staircase they descended led to still more of the same winding passageways and mazelike architecture. True to Aki's scouting report, there was no sign of an ambush. Walking next to them, Lefiya and Filvis were attentively monitoring their surroundings.

...It's almost similar to the upper levels of the Dungeon, Finn mused, eyes narrowing as he took in the height, width, and branching nature of their current passageway. *An orichalcum door in the Old Sewerway...even deeper than the other waterways crossing the city. I'd say we're easily somewhere between the first and second floors of the Dungeon now, given those stairs we just descended.*

In his head, he was already unfolding his mental map of not only the great pit beneath Babel Tower but the first and second floors of the Dungeon, as well. It was enough to convince him that the large-scale labyrinth they were currently navigating was bordering on the Dungeon's uppermost levels.

Putting aside the matter of how, if someone were to somehow connect these halls with the Dungeon, they could feasibly create a separate entrance in addition to Babel. Perhaps it would be safest to assume this entire maze...no, this man-made "labyrinth" is the second entrance to the Dungeon itself.

Finn's eyes dropped to the orderly arrangement of stones that made up the path beneath his feet.

The question, then, is just how deep *this labyrinth goes...*

From the steps they'd taken and time that had passed since their passage through the orichalcum door alone, it was obvious the structure was massive—easily at least as large as the entire sewer system beneath Orario's streets.

But just how far, and how deep, would it continue?

Violas had been born from the twenty-fourth-floor pantry, and Lefiya had witnessed the remnants of the Evils on the eighteenth floor—if Finn's hypothesis was correct, and this maze really did travel as deep as the middle levels...that would truly be an astonishing feat.

Much like Aiz, Finn simply couldn't shake that lingering suspicion gnawing at him.

"...It looks like a room," Aki suddenly murmured as the path in front of them opened up.

The square-shaped space that appeared before them very much resembled the various rooms of the Dungeon. It was wide enough to comfortably fit ten or so adventurers—perhaps fifty meders across?

Orichalcum doors barred the passages to their left and right, while in front of them and directly across from the stairwell was an open path leading forward.

"..."

It was quiet. Unsettlingly so. Almost as if on cue, Bete's ears twitched.

Aki mirrored his reaction, as did the rest of the animal people in the group.

Every eye was drawn to the path in front of them, where a set of unhurried footsteps could be heard echoing off the surrounding walls. Soon, they were joined by a decidedly human-shaped shadow emerging from the darkness.

"Fiiiiiiiiiiiiiiiiiiiiiiiiiiiiinnnnnnnnnnnnnnnnnnnnn!!"

The scream erupted from between the woman's lips the moment she came into view.

It was so loud it was hard to believe it came from a woman, and Raul and the others clapped their hands over their ears.

The source was a human adventurer, looking down at them haughtily.

"Oh, Braver! How I've been dying to see you, you little shit!!" she exclaimed wickedly, spittle flecking her lips.

"Huh. Valletta. I had a hunch you were still alive..." Finn responded with a sharpened gaze of his own.

The woman in the overcoat lined with fur was a wild-looking sort.

At the revelation of her name, Raul and Aki reacted with identical looks of apprehension.

"Not a day's gone by that I've been able to wipe that shit-eating, Mister Cool Guy face of yours outta my mind! You remember me, you bastard?! You start actin' like you forgot and you're dead!! You hear me? I'll rip out your guts, tear off your face, and carve up your little body until you never even think about mouthing off to me ever again!"

She didn't seem to care that they'd been standing in front of each other for barely a moment, forgetting herself and loosing a barrage of obscenities. Her eyes flashed with a devilish light, seeing nothing but *Loki Familia's* prum captain.

"...Yo, Finn. You got some kinda crazy-broad-attractin' disease or somethin'?" Bete scoffed as he directed a look of disgust at the woman in front of them.

"If you're talking about Tione, Bete, then hold your tongue," Finn scolded, even as the eyes of the woman in question continued to bore into him. "At the very least, Tione is human, which is more than I can say for this one." He raised his green eyes to meet her depraved smile.

Those in the group with no recollection of the woman were surprised to see that Finn and the others seemed to know her well.

"You—you know this person, Captain?" the hume bunny Rakuta asked in shock.

"I'm afraid I do. She's known as Valletta Grede, a major player in the Evils' uprising. She helped them upset the order and give rise to Orario's dark age, now fifteen years past," Finn answered without hesitation.

Everyone in the group gasped.

"The captain, Miss Riveria, Mister Gareth…everyone was involved. And not just *Loki Familia*, either. Even *Freya Familia* and *Ganesha Familia* got thrown in the mix," Aki explained, her voice hardened.

"I always assumed she was long dead by the time they stopped Gale Wind's rampage that finished off the last of those Evils five years ago. That means, during the Twenty-Seventh-Floor Nightmare…" Raul added, equally as stiff. *Loki Familia* had naturally been involved in the extermination of the Evils for the past fifteen years. Having joined the familia eight years ago, Raul and Aki were all too familiar with the events that had taken place.

"Yes. She must have merely faked her own death, taking the opportunity to go into hiding," Finn concluded.

"What a little genius we have here! Pisses me off!" Valletta's smile grew more depraved still. "Thanks to you and your bloody Guild friends, we Evils lost a lotta muscle on that day six years ago. So you know what we did, huh? We egged on ol' Olivas and pretended like the whole bunch of us had bought the farm!"

The Twenty-Seventh-Floor Nightmare was a large-scale pass parade instigated by the Evils. They lured in not only every monster on the floor but the floor's Monster Rex, as well, pitting all of them against the ensnared adventurers sent by the Guild. What resulted was a massive battle with nigh uncountable bodies piling up on both sides. Valletta and the other high-level Evils had taken the opportunity to add their own "dead bodies" to the mix, effectively throwing the Guild off their scent in the process.

Everything, including the sacrifices of their brethren, had been for this day when they could rise again. The true purpose of the "nightmare" had been, in fact, to prolong the life of their decaying organization.

However.

"You know what you are, Finn? Scum. Miserable, disgusting scum, the worst of the worst!! Because you didn't go! That day, you didn't try and help on the twenty-seventh floor! Instead, you got intel from somewhere, took Freya's and Ganesha's people, and attacked our gods!" Valletta continued, her voice crackling with a violent energy directed straight at Finn.

And it was true. Finn had seen through the plans of Valletta and her peers and, realizing there wasn't enough time, had simply *abandoned the twenty-seventh floor*. Instead, he had taken his people and attacked every single location that could possibly house the Evils' base. He'd even discerned that their garrison was weak. Together with the help of the other gods, he succeeded in sending a frightening number of the so-called "evil gods" back to the heavens, which had tipped the balance of power between the Evils and the Guild.

All of this made Finn, "Braver," anathema to the remaining Evils.

"Do you even know what it felt like? How terrifying it is to have your god whisked away and your blessing sealed? In the middle of the Dungeon?! I can't even count the number of times some monster or another almost sank its teeth into me!"

"I don't doubt your suffering. However, given everything that you and your friends have done, I can't say I feel any remorse."

"Take your remorse and shove it! I don't even care anymore. Not about the Evils, not about what happened. But you? I'll never forgive you, you pretentious little freak! I promised myself...that I'd pay you back one day for everything you did to me!!" Spit flew from her mouth, and her eyes turned bloodshot as she talked, as if she was reliving the memories of that day. "After I rip off those scrawny little arms and legs, I'm gonna ride you until I've had enough and then turn that self-righteous face into mincemeat!! And then...once I've had my fill...I'm gonna laugh until I can't even breathe!!"

"My, my. Inviting me to a one-night stand?" Finn responded airily to the woman's uncultured taunts. "I dare say, I'm flattered. However, I do apologize. Because of the hopes of my race, I'm only allowed to whisper sweet nothings into the ear of my own kind."

Seeing their captain behave so cool and collected while engaging in what ended up becoming a rather erotic exchange with the hostile woman was enough to make the female members of the group decidedly red-faced and flushed. After all, Tione wasn't the only one with feelings for their beloved prum captain.

"I also might add, though I'm loath to say it to a member of the fairer sex...you'll need to improve your character a bit before asking me out again. At least aim for something along the lines of Riveria's sophistication, hmm?"

"*Eeeee!!*" A squeal arose from the fan club behind him.

"*So he does like Lady Riveria...!!*"

"*I need to write this down!*"

The girls whipped out notebooks from who knows where, completely forgetting their current situation. Meanwhile, the others of the group not completely taken in by Finn's charm or who were otherwise fearful of Tione's fury (the men, Aki, and Lefiya, to name a few) merely rubbed their arms in awkward silence. Bete, on the other hand, realizing Finn's words were solely meant to provoke, wearily hung his head.

"Go to hell, Finn!!" Opposite their group, Valletta's fury was reaching a peak. As veins popped up along her forehead, she shot Finn a look of pure, unadulterated murder. "Oh yeah! I am definitely going to kill you! Here and now!"

"A bit after-the-fact, though, wouldn't you say? If I've really been plaguing your mind so much these years, surely you could have found a better opportunity to off me than this?"

"Ha! Shit for brains! You still don't get it! I've been waiting for you to come down here, completely oblivious, right into our castle! You marched in all according to plan!!" she crowed with a voracious grin, and this time it was enough to wipe the smile from Finn's face. Her eyes were glittering, like a bird about to snatch up its prey, and consumed with revenge, she declared:

"This will be your grave! Let yourself be swallowed in the majesty of Knossos...and *die*!!"

—"Knossos"?

Finn's eyebrows twitched at this. Was that the name of the labyrinth? But before he could think further, Valletta raised her right arm and, with it, a small globe-shaped object. Wrapped in a layer of ingot, its core appeared to be a round red sphere—with a visible *D* carved into its surface. The moment the spherical and apparently magical item gave off a crimson flash, the door behind them rumbled closed.

"W-we're trapped!" Raul cried as, almost instantaneously, the two doors on either side of the room snapped open to reveal identical swarms of violas.

With a smirk at her handiwork, Valetta leaped off the floor and disappeared down the passage behind her.

"Let's get stuck in, you bastards!" Bete howled.

"*Guuuwwwwaaaaaaarrrrrrrggggggghhh!*" The violas followed up with a thunderous roar of their own, signaling the battle's start.

The members of *Loki Familia* readied their respective weapons before launching themselves at the incoming monsters.

That magic item Valletta used...is it the key to the orichalcum doors?...It certainly seemed like she was showing it to us on purpose. As Finn took his place beside Bete and butchered one viola after another with his gold-tipped long spear, he glanced in the direction Valletta had just disappeared. *Bait, then, perhaps? To lure us into the actual trap?...A bait we'll unfortunately be forced to take.*

The violas came in an unceasing flood. And considering their one way out had been effectively cut off, they didn't have much choice other than to press on.

"Everyone, straight ahead!" he instructed, and the other members of the group were quick to obey. They charged forward in perfect alignment, slipping in and out between the rush of giant flowers and speeding toward the far passage.

The violas, naturally, gave chase.

They barreled into the single tunnel, wide enough to accept the adventurers easily, but not so much the large flowers hurling themselves into it with all the force of an avalanche.

"—Captain! Leave them to Miss Filvis and me!" Lefiya shouted as she eyed the situation behind them. The courageous initiative was enough to startle Raul and the others; Finn, however, simply glanced back from his position in the center of the party, meeting Lefiya's azure eyes before affirming her request with a nod.

"They're in your hands, then, Lefiya!"

"Roger!" The trusting smile from her captain gave Lefiya a thrill of excitement as she whirled to face the onrush of violas head-on. "Miss Filvis!"

The elf in question inferred Lefiya's plan from a single glance. "...Understood. Leave them to me!" Filvis replied, taking a step forward and thrusting her left hand outward. "*Shield me, cleansing chalice!*"

The spell was complete in an instant.

"*Dio Grail!!*"

A circular force field was triggered by her short chant. The pure-white light, a symbol of its caster's nobility, instantly transformed into an ironlike shield to protect them from the violas' onslaught.

"*Unleashed pillar of light, limbs of the holy tree. You are the master archer—!*"

Lefiya's voice soared with a spell of its own. Now that Filvis's shield had blocked off the tunnel and the monsters couldn't take a step, she sped effortlessly through the chant she knew by heart, weaving a cannon of light into existence.

"Now, Miss Filvis!" she screamed, giving the other elf just enough time to retract her shield spell and step out of the way before launching her own magic in its place.

"*Arcs Ray!!*"

"―――――――*GWOOOOAAAGGHH?!*"

The flash of dazzling light washed through the entire passageway, swallowing all the violas in a shining river. The point-blank attack cremated them on contact, effectively purging the entire swarm.

"These...these tactics are practically Dungeon worthy...!" Lefiya muttered in awe.

"Yes, we'll have plenty more time to practice them there if we make it out of here alive. Stay on guard. More on their way!" Filvis commented as the next wave approached. The two elves called forth their magic circles a second time to fend off the attacks as a pair.

"D-did you see that? Lefiya's amazing!"

"Well, when you don't have to worry about more monsters spawning from the walls, it certainly gives you more room to work with."

Raul and Aki, two higher-level adventurers, were legitimately impressed with Lefiya's tactical expertise.

"...Heh, so she's finally gone and made herself useful, has she?" Bete smirked, offering his own two cents on Lefiya's tangible growth.

"Exceeding our expectations is all we can ask of the next generation." Finn gave a smile of his own. His voice sharpened as he returned to the situation at hand. "Bete! Stay up front! Take out anything in our path! But don't stray too far—we don't want to stretch our numbers too thin!"

Bete was quick to respond, leading the rest of the front line toward the shadows emerging from the darkness up ahead.

"Those aren't violas...! Then, a new species?!"

The monsters that came into view resembled water spiders. They were tall—coming up to a human's waist, in fact—and boasted six long legs. Strange red crystals, different from magic stones, could be seen embedded in their central bodies—small but impossibly numerous.

Having been shuffled into the forward party, the hume bunny Rakuta hesitated for a moment, unsure what kind of attack they should even expect from these never-before-seen beasts.

"Does it matter? Just take 'em out before they even think about attackin'!"

"Gwuuoogh?!"

Bete sprinted forward and tore through the spiders in one fell swoop. Their bodies were reduced to shreds as Bete's razor-sharp boots sliced through them like butter. True to his word, he hadn't even allowed the monsters a chance to go on the offensive. It was the sort of feat only the most powerful of adventurers could pull off, one that elicited trembling awe from his peers as they fell in line behind him.

Meanwhile, back in the party's center...

"Whuuaah! A pitfall!" Raul gave a shout as he leaped backward while Bete fielded the attacks ahead.

"Careful! There's more around it, too!" Aki warned, and true enough, square holes of roughly five meders across had begun to open all along the passage floor.

The pitch-black gloom emanating from the shafts was evidence enough as to their great depth; however, they appeared not to be purposefully laid traps but abandoned efforts at expansion. Equipped with her buckler and light sword, Aki paid close attention to the ground underfoot as Raul unsheathed his bow and arrow next to her, aiming at the creepy-crawlies now coming out of the woodwork on either side.

*She's watching us...*Finn noted with a glance at his surroundings, flourishing his spear from his spot in the middle of the group. He'd gone up against the Evils enough times at this point to be all too familiar with Valletta's inclinations—she hadn't fled. No, she'd hidden somewhere in the grand architecture of the labyrinth and was now monitoring them closely, no doubt just waiting for the perfect opportunity to launch her trap—

Finn's head stopped mid-scan when a massive crossroads came into view.

All of a sudden, his thumb was throbbing out of control.

"_____"

It was pain sharper than he'd ever felt before.

An omen fierce enough to make his fingers twitch.

It was then that Finn heard it.

The sound of a door rumbling open nearby.

This is...

Even for someone with a sixth sense for danger like Finn, this was too much, too fast.

There was no time to give orders. His body simply couldn't react fast enough. This was an Irregular neither he nor the rest of the party had the capacity to suppress. The type of Irregular he'd already lost countless men to on expeditions to the Dungeon's depths.

The fear of impending doom descended over him with chills like a frigid winter.

When suddenly, from immediately to his side…

The entire pack of hellish beasts parted in a single flash of movement.

Almost as though opening a path for their revered king.

They revealed the door at the end of the crossroads, now open, and a figure cut through the shadow—

—That red hair.

Green eyes, an eerie black longsword, and hair the color of freshly spilled blood.

All at once, the figure disappeared.

An instant later, the creature, Levis, was directly in front of Finn.

"Ngh?!"

"So we meet again, prum."

The frosty voice descended upon him at the same time as her obsidian sword.

She followed through even as he blocked the strike, nearly blasting him backward from the incredible shock.

She had power, speed, and a destructive force more powerful than his small body could take.

After only three crosses of the blade, his strength simply *gave out.*

"This is payback. For what happened on the eighteenth floor."

Her intimidating aura was worlds apart from that of their previous encounter. And her combat ability was *nigh unthinkable.*

She was not only a creature but an enhanced species.

Just how many magic stones had she eaten—?

—It's Hell Finegas or nothing.

He had to use it or he'd lose.

But just as this thought floated through his head, so did a sudden sense of foreboding.

Yes, his patented Berserker spell would increase his abilities by leaps and bounds, but it would also saturate his mind with a lust for blood, transforming him into a battle-thirsty warrior incapable of issuing orders.

If Raul and the rest of his party were forced to fend for themselves in a situation like this...

As the party's leader, he paused for one anguished moment at the thought.

A moment that proved fatal.

"Die."

The mere instant of hesitation was like a massive opening for Levis as she was now.

Her sword carved a ravenous arc through the air before connecting with Finn's body.

"Gngh—!"

It divided the handle of his spear as he attempted to raise it in defense, before finally plunging into his tiny frame.

Finn's world turned red. As blood clouded his vision, he saw Levis's unimpressed features disappear from view. Behind him, no one uttered a sound. Time slowed to a dull crawl as both his Fortia Spear and body jerked backward.

"Ca..."

The rest of the party was powerless to so much as react as their beloved Braver slowly fell.

"...*Captaaaaaaaiiiiiiiiiiiiinnnnnnn!!*"

His body bounced as it hit the ground amid the cries of his party members.

First Bete, then Lefiya spun around at the commotion, and time froze.

Finn had fallen.

Braver, the one who had always roused the familia back to its feet no matter the situation, had fallen.

They had seen Riveria, Gareth, and themselves taste defeat before, but *Loki Familia* had never felt a despair like this. It was an unfathomable blow. Their panic had swelled in an instant, threatening to burst and restart time.

There was no one to replace him.

Finn was *Loki Familia*'s emotional fulcrum. The one person who simply *couldn't crumble.*

Which was why...

Finn understood better than anyone, faster than anyone, just how calamitous the current situation really was.

The drop in morale. The confusion. The utter collapse of the group.

All of it culminated into a few words in his blood-clouded thoughts: *We'll be wiped out.*

It triggered the fastest decision he'd ever made.

"Raul!!"

Ignoring his blood-soaked body, Finn called out to a single young man frozen in fear.

After all the knowledge and experience he'd learned the hard way from Finn and the other elites over the years, Raul understood immediately, leaping into action before Finn even had to tell him what to do.

"!!"

Tossing aside his bow and arrow, he flew. Faster than Levis. Faster than anyone.

With no one but Finn in his sights, he ran forward at breakneck speed, and not even the flash of Levis's sword deterred him.

That single decisive action would prove victorious.

He extended his arms, still trembling with the shock, right shoulder still mangled from their previous bout, and *caught him.*

Levis cursed under her breath.

But Raul didn't stop. Cradling the prum's small frame like an infant, he pushed off the ground with everything he had, streaking toward the far passage—and toward the abyssal void of the nearest pitfall.

"Follow me!!"

"!"

Aki and the others heeded his desperate yell and quickly fell in line behind him.

Abandoning the battle at hand, they dove down the pit, escaping the wrath of the creature and her monster brethren.

Finn and the rest of the party's center had fled.

"Bwa-ha-ha-ha-ha-ha-ha-ha!!"

Valletta's laughter resounded off the narrow walls of the tunnel.

As Finn had surmised earlier, she had been secretly observing the party's progress. Now, after poking her head out from one of the side passages, she made her way toward the pitfall Raul and the others had just dropped into.

"How do you like that, huh, Finn?! Run, run away with your tail between your legs like the miserable dog you are! It makes for a wonderful show!" she shouted gleefully down the length of the chasm before turning her gaze to Levis. "That was some quality work. Guess you picked the right profession, eh, Miss Kill for Hire?"

"The head's gone now," the red-haired creature woman replied in annoyance, glancing down the hole. It was no longer her concern. "From here on out, I follow Aria."

"H-hey! But Finn is still—"

"Do the rest yourself. Or do I need to serve him to you on a silver platter?"

Levis responded coldly, giving her sword a flick. The prum's blood still painted its black blade, sliding down the side to color the ground with tiny spatters.

Without another word, she turned on her heel to chase her own target.

"Screw you, too, then...Creep." Valletta made a face in disgust at the departing woman. "But whatever! Like I care! I don't want anyone else to have the pleasure of killin' him anyway. Don't go too far now, Fiiiiiinn! I'll be over in just a moment to bring you down!"

Her annoyance soon faded in favor of a sadistic smile as she gazed toward the hole. The wicked twist of her lips made her obsession clear to any who saw it.

"...You...bastards..."

But the voice this time was the decidedly husky growl of a certain werewolf. As the first of the stunned-silent front line to recover from his shock, Bete leaped forward toward the woman, eyes flashing.

"Ruuuuuuuuuuuaaaaaaaaaaaaarrrrtrrrrrrgggggggghhhhhhhhhh!!"

His enraged howl echoed off the walls as he went flying toward his enemies. Tearing through the monsters standing in his way, leaving dust in his wake, he stretched his claws toward Valletta, but...

"You're seriously attacking me head-on? At Level Six? Be real, Vanargand." Valletta laughed before again thrusting forward her spherical magic item. Rather than giving off a brilliant light as it had the time before, it instead triggered the thick metal wall immediately in front of Bete to drop with a sudden *thud*.

"!!"

The crossroad disappeared from in front of him, replaced by the all-too-familiar sight of an orichalcum door blocking his way. Seeing the impenetrable obstacle before him, Bete could do nothing but roar in anger.

"*Shit!!*"

There was a terrible *thud* as his fist hit the door, but the orichalcum held strong.

He ground his teeth together audibly, his blue tattoo contorting on his face.

"M-Mister Bete!"

As if this new barrier weren't enough, the frightened screams of his allies behind him alerted him to an all-new danger. He whirled around, coming face-to-face with a teeming throng of everything from water spiders to violas.

Presents from Valletta, huh? Bete cursed beneath his breath at the enemy's trap as he quickly surveyed the situation. The tunnel they were currently occupying had been effectively turned into a cage, and they were the rats. Even if Bete himself would emerge unscathed from the horde, there was no way his fellow familia members would.

As much as it pained him, they had no choice but to retreat.

"We're gettin' the hell outta here!" he shouted.

The party was quick to respond, powering through the wave of monsters in desperate retreat. Bete could do nothing but join them in leaving the door behind.

"C-Captain...Mister Bete..."

Lefiya was powerless as she watched the events play out. Though she'd successfully stopped the violas behind her, she hadn't been able to move from her position. She and Filvis, who'd stayed in the back to protect their rear, were all alone now, effectively separated from the rest of the party.

Valletta glanced at the two frozen elves.

"Hey, Miss Kill for Hire. At least take care of those two elves, would ya? I have to go pay a visit to the tear-stricken face of a certain high-and-mighty prum." With that, she closed the last door, and the intersection was completely sealed off.

Now that she had cut off all means of support for Finn, Valletta let her laughter fade on the far side of the wall.

Levis looked none too happy about the last-minute duty thrust upon her, no doubt anxious to exact her own revenge, but she turned toward Lefiya and Filvis all the same.

Lefiya's shoulders gave a jump at the icy gaze that met hers.

"..."

Levis's eyes narrowed ever so slightly.

Then, she simply turned away, *completely ignoring them* and continuing on her own path.

"Wha—?"

—*She let us go!*

Had she deemed them unworthy of her time? Lefiya felt a tiny fire begin to grow in the pit of her stomach with a sharp crackle.

There was another rumble from the direction Levis had left.

Leaping into action, Lefiya raced after her, only to see the red-haired woman already gone behind the newly closed door.

"Gngh...!" Lefiya bit down on her lip in frustration.

"Lefiya, wait! Calm down!" Filvis called out as she jogged to catch up.

The sound of the other elf's voice was enough to restore her composure somehow, and her ragged breathing finally slowed.

"Miss Filvis, the others, we...we must save them...!"

"I know, but the way is blocked. There'll be no getting through those orichalcum doors, no matter how much you want to help Braver...!"

There was an urgency to Filvis's voice. Even Lefiya could pick up on it.

The room behind them had already been shut off; those impervious doors of steel blocked their routes to Finn, Bete, and the others. Lefiya and Filvis were truly and utterly alone, trapped in the middle of this giant labyrinth.

"Then...then what are we supposed to do? Try and find them? Try to escape, get word to Lady Riveria and the others? Either way, we're—"

"We'll find a new route." Filvis cut through Lefiya's rant with a nod, her features strained. "Come. We'll need to do our best to avoid combat. Though I fear we're already deep within the spider's web..."

If that was the case, they'd need to find themselves their own version of the ariadne guides.

Swallowing hard, Lefiya nodded.

Then, the two elves sped toward one of the passage's side tunnels, seeking out their one sliver of hope.

"_____"

Snap.

Gareth stopped with a start at the sudden, unbidden crack that formed along the back of his gauntlet.

"Gareth...? What's wrong?" Aiz asked from behind him.

"...Nothing. Ain't nothing," Gareth replied before turning around. Glancing back at the path Finn and the others had taken, he attempted to shake off the lingering feeling of dread tugging at the hairs on the back of his neck.

Unease aside, he had no choice but to continue forward.

"This place is..."

"...huge..."

Tione and Tiona murmured in awe.

The spot they'd reached was almost exactly the same as the large hall Finn and his party had arrived at not long ago. There was only a single exit, positioned straight ahead and just slightly above their current vantage point. It was around the same height as a building's second floor, only with no stairs, making it a curious structural design.

Before the twins' comments even had a chance to fade away, the figure of a man appeared from the passage in front of them.

"!"

"A pleasure to finally meet you...adventurers of *Loki Familia*."

The light of the magic-stone lanterns illuminated the features of a lugubrious-looking man emerging from the shadows. He wore a set of loose-fitting work clothes topped by a long waistcloth; his weary and begrimed appearance was the antithesis of clean. His sickly pale skin told of a life away from the light of day, and his washed-out, almost desaturated hair hung down in unkempt clumps, hiding one of his eyes. Beneath its visible counterpart was a large, dark bag.

There was no question about it. While time had certainly passed since the deed had been done, he was, without doubt—

"—The guy from the picture!"

"Yeah, you're the human who made that deal with the sea god in Meren, aren't you?"

As Tiona pointed at him, Tione's tone was considerably sharper than her sister's.

The man in question glanced downward at the two Amazonian

twins. "Something like that happened, yes...You said you were look-ing for me? However, I've certainly had no interest in meeting you," he remarked, so softly it might as well have been a whisper.

Tiona and Tione blinked in confusion.

"At any rate, even meeting like this costs me precious time. The will of our ancestors is grand, indeed. There is never enough...Even were we to one day complete it, there's no guarantee I will be around to bear witness. This human body is a truly odious thing...Even with the boon of elven blood. Ah, a pity, really..."

As he muttered his mystifying soliloquy, he drew the attention of not just the twins but the rest of the party, including Aiz. Was he really about to simply wave them along? *Loki Familia*? His enemy?

Considering the remnants of the Evils were usually coming at them with everything they had, this man was a rather unusual specimen.

"H-h-h-hey now! Stay with us, would ya? No flyin' away to la-la land!"

"Yeah, what the hell is wrong with you? What do you even want?!"

The twins' indignant shouts brought the man's monologue to a halt, and he lifted his gaze. "I do apologize. I am called...Barca. Nothing more," he replied in the same dispirited tone. It was an honest answer, though the man's eye narrowed with mild irritation. "I've been tasked with luring you deeper into the shadows of the abyss..."

At these words, a spark of tension ran through the group. The healer Leene, Cruz, and the rest of the party readied their weapons. As for Gareth, still silent at the front of the pack, he had noticed a troubling discrepancy:

There's no way this spindly stalk of a man's alone, is there? Aiz and them could cut 'im down in an instant given the chance. And there's no sign of any monsters lurkin' about...

The man, Barca, was clearly not a fighter. A mage or hexer, per-haps. But even then, the moment he tried to unleash a spell, Aiz or someone would stop him in his tracks—at this distance, even a quick chant couldn't beat their speed.

If the enemy was hoping to take on their party, they were severely lacking in men. Yet, there were still no signs of a monster ambush.

Which could mean only one thing: This dispassionate man currently exchanging words with them—was setting a trap.

———?

It was at this moment that something caught Gareth's eye.

A red orb…in the middle o' the floor…?

It was embedded in the center of the stone hall, a jewel not dissimilar to the many they'd already seen as they made their way through the maze—just decidedly bigger.

"‼"

Gareth suddenly looked upward with a gasp.

Barca's eyes were focused solely on the jewel.

As if on cue, something inside the stone began to *thrum*.

"Everyone, ju—"

"You're too late."

Interrupting Gareth's warning cry, Barca swept forward his bangs to reveal his left eye.

An eye of red—emblazoned with the letter *D*.

In that instant.

KA-THWOOM.

The floor around them simply *opened up*.

"_____"

Aiz, Tiona, Tione, Gareth, and the rest of the party froze.

Suddenly with no ground beneath their feet, they found themselves floating in the air above a boundless chasm of darkness.

It was a pitfall.

The stone that had been supporting them wasn't an ordinary floor at all.

In fact, it wasn't even stone but a material they'd become all too familiar with at this point in their dungeon crawl: orichalcum.

Two orichalcum doors of monstrous proportions, disguised as a floor.

It was a Dungeon Gimmick. And it had just swung open beneath their feet.

"Farewell, *Loki Familia*...and sweet dreams."

They fell.

"Whhhhuuuuuuuuuuuuaaaaaaaa*aaaaaaaaaaaaaaaaaaa*hhhhhhhhh!!"

All they could do was scream as their bodies plunged into the darkness.

It was a trap that spanned the entire room. A trap that Barca had unlocked to ensnare every adventurer of *Loki Familia*'s party.

"A pitfall?!"

"Damn it!"

As Tiona let out a surprised scream, Tione and a number of others pulled out ropes and chains anchored to knives or claws, launching them at the wall. But the sturdy, seamless surface of adamantite repelled the incoming weapons. The chasm would allow them to do nothing but fall—a revelation that filled the party's eyes with terror.

Even first-tier adventurers were rendered powerless without firm ground to stand on.

Their minds went blank with shock and confusion as above them, the twin orichalcum doors slowly, mercilessly rumbled shut.

"Aiz!"

"Ngh!"

Almost in sync with each other, Gareth and Aiz leaped into motion.

"Guurraaagh!!"

"*Awaken, Tempest!!*"

Gareth flung his ax toward Aiz as the wind swirled up around her. She slammed her sword into the oncoming weapon to propel herself skyward and, drawing power from her Airiel, ascended at an astonishing speed. Just as the doors were about to grind to a close, she shot up through the shrinking gap, the sole person to escape from the trap.

"?!"

In fact, it launched her so high that she made it all the way to the second floor of the room, landing in front of a very surprised Barca in one continuous leap.

Barca stepped backward, putting distance between himself and the Sword Princess. "Now, this is a surprise...I hadn't expected anyone would be able to escape my ancestor's trap."

"Open these doors, *now!*" Aiz ordered, her friends' peril at the forefront of her mind.

Barca's one visible eye narrowed ever so slightly. "But I cannot allow myself to be caught."

He had only one escape route.

As he took off down the path behind him, Aiz was hot on his heels. She would have caught him, too, had another orichalcum door not slammed down with a shudder the moment Barca scampered through a nearby side tunnel.

"Gngh...?!" Aiz cursed, glaring at the irritating obstruction before turning back toward the hall. Standing where Barca had only a few moments earlier, she gazed into the empty room.

"I'll find you...!"

Meanwhile, in the dark recesses of the labyrinth.

"Are we...trapped...?"

"We lost Gareth and Aiz, too..."

Tione, Tiona, and the rest of the group attempted to peer through the darkness at the bottom of the pit.

"Gareth, what do we do...?!"

"I'm afraid the tables have turned, lads 'n' lasses. We may have started as the hunters, but we're most certainly the hunted now. Buck up!" Gareth replied as he donned his helmet to face the writhing mob of monsters that had already formed around them.

"Captain! *Captain!!*"

"...Ra...ul...Give the order to...retreat..." Finn managed, his breath growing increasingly labored as blood continued to gush from his wound.

Raul and his companions could only cry out in teary-eyed despair at the sight of their half-dead captain.

Still wrapped in Raul's arms, Finn rolled his eyes weakly toward the shadowed ceiling, eyelids fluttering closed.

"Which way, Mister Bete...?!"

"The hell am I supposed to know?! Use your damn nose! Or your ears! I don't care how; just find a way to Finn!" Bete shouted back at his animal-person peers as the group made their way aimlessly through the maze.

"Lefiya! We'll make for the exit first. It must be here somewhere!"

"R-right!"

At the same time, Lefiya and Filvis frantically navigated their own way down the convoluted passages in an effort to deliver the rest of their companions from their current predicament.

Meanwhile.

"The Sword Princess may have escaped...but all is as Thanatos planned."

Barca had successfully evaded his assailant and was now ambling unaccompanied down the dark passageway.

"No doubt Valletta and the others have also succeeded in their duties. The preparations are complete..."

Door after door opened before his red eye, the key to the maze, allowing him free rein of the labyrinth. Softly, he made his declaration.

"You shall become the cornerstone of my ancestor's greatest work, *Loki Familia*...the man-made dungeon Knossos."

The darkness bared its fangs.

FEAST OF THE DEAD

Гэта казка іншага сям'і.

◆

фестываль смерці

"No good! The door's closed…We can't get inside!"

The scream of one of the lower-level members echoed off the stone of the hidden passageway outside the maze. This new development was enough to stir the others in the group—Riveria and the rest of *Loki Familia*, currently stationed outside the main door—into a frenzy.

It had already been seven hours since Finn and his team had entered the labyrinth, which, combined with the radio silence beyond the door, was enough to confirm that something had happened.

"They're trapped in there, then…Not entirely unexpected, but what are you thinkin', Riveria?"

"They could be separated by all the orichalcum doors in the world, and Gareth would still be able to break through the adamantite walls if worse came to worst. The fact that he hasn't done so…leads me to believe they've gotten themselves caught in a trap," Riveria mused, staring into the darkness. "It's not like them to miscalculate the ideal time for retreat." Her jade-colored eyes narrowed sharply as she glanced around at her frightened companions.

"Right. Lemme put it this way, then: If they really have taken a tumble down a pitfall…will they be able to get themselves out?" Loki asked.

"Were this an ordinary maze, I'd say yes without question. However…" She trailed off, stepping toward the nearby wall and giving it a sharp rap with the butt end of her staff to expose the underlying gleam of adamantite. She scooped up a piece of the fallen stone in her hand. "Just as I thought…"

"Whazzat? It mixed with somethin' weird?"

"Indeed. Obsidian soldier matter."

As Loki peeped over curiously, Riveria responded by naming the drop item.

Obsidian soldiers were a type of rock monster that appeared on the thirty-seventh floor of the Dungeon. Boasting bodies of magic-repellent rock, they had the ability to severely reduce the effects of any magic spell cast at them. The drop item for these lapidary beasts went for a pretty penny up on the surface and was often used to make superior-grade, magic-resistant shields and armor.

"I can only assume it's blended into the entirety of the stone face covering the adamantite, making it not only solid but magic-resistant, as well," she continued before crushing the chunk of anti-magic obsidian between her slender white fingers. Her brows furrowed. "Meaning, were I to attack from the outside, I would only cause damage to Daedalus Street and the sewerway. If not even I am capable of breaking in, I can only imagine the labor it would necessitate from the inside...Finn's spear, too, is likely useless," she finished coolly. The rest of the group gulped anxiously.

"You serious?" Loki's eyes widened ever so slightly as she turned a glance toward the maze.

"The labyrinth we're currently facing is nigh unprecedented. I know not what led to its creation...What I can say for certain, though, is that it's based on a sort of deep-rooted belief far beyond what we can even imagine," Riveria asserted, laying to rest their previous theories that this dungeon was merely an enemy stronghold.

Following this assumption, the high elf and goddess began actively attempting a plan of action.

"Hmm...Riveria? Your magic circle. Didn't it have, like, some kinda radar thingamajig to it?" Loki asked.

"While I'm not sure what a 'radar thingamajig' is...if you're speaking of my Rae Laevateinn, it can, indeed, discern whether humans or monsters are within its magic circle. However, the effect is merely horizontal. I can't guarantee it will work on floors below us."

"How about this: You make the biggest damn magic circle you can but cancel it out before the flames start comin', and just...do it over and over again? Wasteful and inefficient as hell, I know, but it's worth a shot. At least we can check out this floor, yeah?"

"Understood. I'll give it a try," the mage responded before quickly beginning her chant.

As the massive jade-colored magic circle formed beneath her feet, Loki quickly began issuing out further orders. "Alicia! Grab a few people and start whippin' up a map! I have absolutely zero clue how big this place is gonna turn out to be, but we're gonna use that magic circle to find out!"

"R-roger!" the elf acknowledged before calling out to her peers for help.

Loki grimly watched her go as the brilliant green glow from Riveria's magic circle bathed her body in light.

Soft blue phosphorescence illuminated the faces of the two figures shrouded in darkness.

"*Loki Familia* has fallen to the eighth floor, just as you instructed."

"Thank you, Barca dear. You've been a wonderful help."

Barca and his god, Thanatos, had met up and begun their conversation.

They were in one of the labyrinth's many rooms, at a depth far below their intruders. Around them lay strewn a ghastly assortment of swords and spears, and from the numerous exits, robed figures wandered in and out. It was the Evils' lair, having been annexed onto the maze post-completion. It was bathed in shadow, scarcely a magic-stone lantern in sight, just the way Thanatos liked it.

"I have to step out for a bit. You'll take care of your little operation for me, won't you?"

"As you wish..."

Barca watched as Thanatos vacated the room, then made his way toward a certain pedestal. Though fashioned out of stone, it resembled the stump of a tree, overgrown with layers of ivy and practically fused with the vegetation itself. Atop it lay a watery film of bluish white, reminiscent of the moon, and a crimson jewel had been affixed to the front of the structure, similar to those embedded in the labyrinth's orichalcum doors, though roughly a size larger.

This was the device. The most important device in the entire maze.

Only Barca and a select few others could operate it.

"—Knossos is certainly lively today."

One of those special few appeared from a side passage.

The voice belonged to a tall, well-built human. One glance at his churlish smile was all it would take to identify him as a scoundrel, and masking his eyes was a pair of smoky quartz goggles. His left eye, the same red as Barca's, was just barely visible through the black lenses.

"Up to somethin', bro?"

"Leave me be, Dix." Barca's annoyance was palpable as he shot his unwelcome guest a look of disdain. "And don't call me that. Not even in jest. We may share the same mother, but that is all."

"Just havin' a little fun is all! You think I'd actually wanna be related to slaves to the curse like you? Makes me sick just thinkin' about it," scoffed the man called Dix.

Barca turned back to the pedestal without another word, uninterested.

"Anyway, the hell is goin' on here today? How're we supposed to sneak those creepy-crawlies out with all this yellin' and screamin'?"

"*Loki Familia* is here…looking for us."

"Whoa, whoa, whoa…hold on there! Yer tellin' me we got some new asswipes comin' for us?"

Images began to appear in the watery film atop the pedestal: deserted passageways at first, then shots of Aiz's harried face as she rushed down a flight of stairs, then Tiona and Tione glancing around in the darkness. Bluish-white flowers had been hidden all about the labyrinth, within the macabre eyes of the maze statues and among

© Kiyotaka Haimura

the reliefs depicting plants on the walls. They were similar to the ones that had sprung up all over the mutated twenty-fourth-floor pantry after the giant parasitic flower appeared. These new blossoms reflected scenes from all over Knossos onto the pedestal's screen of water. Levis and the other creatures had introduced the technology to the man-made labyrinth.

"Perfect. Lend me a hand, Dix?"

"Huh?"

"Thanks to Valletta's negligence, we've got an escaped wolf and fairy on our hands. Look at them, scurrying about…They should be dealt with properly, as our ancestor would wish."

"That's what the monsters and that creature lady are for, yeah? Let them deal with it."

"Unfortunately, that deplorable monstrosity of a woman has gone rogue…It's highly unlikely she'll answer to anyone."

The scene in the water changed to show first a werewolf, drop-kicking a number of monsters that had appeared in his path, followed by two elves racing down a tunnel, and finally to a silently slinking Levis.

"If this keeps up, not only will our underground monster transportation efforts fail, your unsightly hobby would likely be affected, as well…" Barca continued, meeting Dix's gaze.

Dix was silent for a moment, then laughed. "All right, all right. You convinced me. Can't say getting involved with *Loki Familia*'s ever been high on my bucket list, but…what can ya do? This is our home, after all. And the odds are definitely on our side," Dix agreed, his voice crackling with laughter. He knew all too well how unforgiving Knossos could be. "Gimme a new spear, then. I was here to get one anyway. Got a little too wild with the last one and busted it."

"…They're over there. Take whatever you like."

"Heh, I'd expect nothin' less from a wielder of the Mystery ability. You always come prepared, O Great Hexer." Dix grabbed a spear from among its brethren leaning against the wall. It was a long red spear, its tip a twisted point. And while its shape was already nefarious enough, it was the deep bloodred color that truly evoked the curse rippling through it.

Giving the unsettling weapon a few test swings, Dix tapped the handle against his shoulder in apparent approval.

"I'll be off, then. Got me some *Loki Familia* to hunt."

"Captain! Captain, open your eyes!!"

The frightened screams reverberated off the walls of the labyrinth.

Having fallen roughly six floors of the upper levels, Raul, Aki, and three others had somehow managed to escape Levis's wrath and were currently attending to a critically injured Finn.

"It's no use, Raul. Nothing is working."

"But why?! We've given him so many potions already! So how come…how come…?!" Raul sputtered, watching as his colleagues administered item after item to their barely conscious captain.

No matter how many they used, Finn's wounds refused to heal. Red rivulets continued to trace their way down his body, taking his life with them, and his small chest was fluttering up and down with shallow breaths—evidence that he was holding on, if only by a thread—and his green eyes stared blurry and unfocused toward the ceiling.

"A curse…!" Aki bit down hard on her lip as she watched their attempts.

"A curse? But…but from where? And when?! If there'd been a weird spell or whatever, it would have gotten us, too…!"

"Think for a moment, Raul! The sword that woman was using! It was definitely Superior-grade. And probably cursed, too!"

Aki had identified the long, malevolent-looking jet-black sword they'd seen Levis holding.

"A cursed sword…" Raul shuddered at the revelation, the rest of their peers, too, paling in fear.

A Superior imbued with a curse: no doubt the work of some hexer, as opposed to a mage, making for a heinous weapon. Cursed weapons were rare enough already, but for the weapon itself to be a Superior made it all the more extraordinary. As for the hex, it was likely an Unhealable Curse—preventing those it afflicted from receiving treatment.

"Then...then, the captain...?!"

"I'm afraid so. Unless we can break the curse, our items and magic are useless..." Aki lamented, causing Raul to fall to his knees.

It was true, then: Finn's condition wasn't going to improve. And if they didn't break the curse quickly, he'd never wake up.

They had nothing they could use. No items. No healers. Which meant—

"We have to get him out of here...!" Aki declared.

Raul's face went from pale to pure white. Escape? From this hellhole teeming with cruel enemies and monsters? Without Finn? They had no idea where they were and no ability to map it out, either. If they couldn't even locate themselves, how were they supposed to find the exit? They had no one to help them. Not Aiz. Not Gareth. Not any of the others. Their chances of survival might as well have been nil.

How in the world were they supposed to do this? Alone, no less!

"Raul! Raul, look at me!"

"!"

The feeling of Aki's hands on his shoulders jolted Raul from his thoughts, his head popping upward.

"We have to save the captain! Not Aiz. Not anyone else. Us. We're the only ones he's got!"

"Aki..."

"So don't...don't let me lose you, too...Not now...!"

Aki's hands were trembling.

Aki was the one with the level head, who was always able to keep her cool no matter how much Raul and the others came apart at the seams, and even she was having trouble containing her panic. It was all she could do to keep her head above water.

And somehow, seeing her attempt to hide her own fragility brought Raul back to his senses.

But still. Still. Still.

—Captain, what should I do?

© Kiyotaka Haimura

Raul threw a desperate glance down at Finn, whose breath was scarcely more than a whisper. Around and around his thoughts raced; the more he struggled to find an answer, the more hopeless their situation seemed.

"Oh, Fiiiiiiiiiiiiiiiiiinn! Where AAAAAAARE yoooooooooooou?"

"!"

The loud, echoing voice cut through Raul's thoughts like a knife. His shoulders jumped, and he spun around, realizing in horror that Valletta was on her way to finish the job Levis had started.

They moved quickly to put their landing spot behind them. Eluding their enemies was top priority at the moment, even with the risks that came from haphazard progression through the labyrinth's passages—if Levis or Valletta caught them, getting lost would be the least of their worries.

Valletta was still a good distance away...but if the thunderous footsteps accompanying her were any indication, she had a whole army with her.

"Don't go dying before I find you! Wouldn't want you to kick the bucket before I SLAUGHTER all your little followers right before your eyes! Ha-ha-ha-ha-ha-ha!!"

"...!"

The sadistic screams stirred a terror within them that drove them onward even faster.

"Keep running!" Raul shouted, the only thing he could do as the situation deteriorated around them.

"Wonderful little trap we've gotten ourselves caught in here..."

"What do we dooooo, Tioneeeeee?!"

Meanwhile, in another corner of the maze, Tione and Tiona were attempting to lead their shaken comrades through the darkness.

"This isn't like the Dungeon at all! Where *are* we?! Hey, we're in major trouble, aren't we?!"

"Calm down! We lose our heads, and we'll only be playing right into their plans!" Tione shouted behind her in an attempt to hide her own anxiety.

The large-scale trap they'd succumbed to had been specifically arranged to target them, a party without Finn's keen intuition to keep them out of harm's way. Their enemy was clearly well prepared with any number of impromptu plans they could deploy practically anywhere in the labyrinth at a moment's notice.

Was Finn okay? And the other group?

I have a bad feeling about this but...You're fine, right, Captain?

Tione told herself she had no reason to worry about someone who was far stronger than she was despite her worries. However, as if in direct opposition to her thoughts, a giant mass of metal came crashing down behind her with a sudden *thud*.

"Wh-what the—?!"

An orichalcum door had effectively split the path in two.

And it had taken Tiona and three in her group with it.

"Tiona? Tiona!! Goddammit!!"

Now the party was even further divided. They hadn't even noticed the door in the darkness. All she had with her now was the animal person Cruz and one of the male supporters.

Cursing her ineptitude, she threw an angry punch at the steely door before taking a look at her surroundings.

Somebody had to have brought that door down, right?! Then where the hell are they?!

The door had closed with such perfect timing that someone must have manually triggered it, which meant they were watching. As Cruz and the other supporter fretted next to her, Tione scanned the dark tunnel and its ominous statues with distrust—before hurling one of her throwing knives *straight at her companion*.

The Filuka knife sailed through the air at an alarming speed.

Her companion, the male supporter, stood frozen in shock at the glinting blade flying his way—then it grazed the side of his cheek as it passed by and plunged straight into the body of the figure hidden behind him.

"Gwuuaagh?!"

"...Huh?"

"An enemy!"

Tione readied her Kukri knives—Zolas this time—and her target fell to the ground as the poor supporter was, once again, shocked into silence. As her companions quickly fell back, Tione moved forward to take their place and launch herself at the swarm of writhing forms in the shadow up ahead.

"M-Miss Tione!"

"Cruz! Olba! Gimme some light!" she shouted, not even looking back as she sent her Zolas screaming through the air. It connected with flesh, and she heard a moan. Behind her, Cruz and Olba pointed their portable magic-stone lanterns toward the darkened area to reveal a company of black-robed figures.

"When did th-they...?!" they sputtered with horror, neither of them able to believe his eyes.

Tione, however, just plowed through their new guests one after another.

These don't look like the Evils Lefiya mentioned...Assassins, then?

Loose-fitting clothes enveloped their bodies beneath their hoods. There was almost something familiar about them—their shadowy presences and gaits were similar to those of the countless assassins she'd run into during her post-Telskyura travels.

Hired hands, then? Or simply a different group of Evils? Either way, Tione wasn't going to let them live.

But suddenly.

"Ngh!"

She was assaulted by a brilliant light—magic, perhaps—as a shrill, high-pitched sound filled the tunnel. Between the limited space and her entanglement with the silent figures, not even her first-tier abilities were enough for her to avoid the attack. Clamping a hand down on one ear, she searched furiously for the source, and she was just about to sidestep an incoming knife when she felt a curious sensation wash over her body.

Why do I...feel so heavy all of a sudden...?!

Her hands, too, were shaking, her motor functions strangely dulled.

In the middle of their own fight in front of the orichalcum door,

Cruz and Olba seemed to realize something before letting out identical moans.

"It—it's a curse! And...anti-Status Magic...!"

The Demerit curse hindered their movement, while the anti-Status Magic lowered their Statuses. The curse was the cause of the feeling of fatigue. Her enemies had essentially sapped her strength.

"Miss Tione! This is really bad!" Cruz shouted in a vain attempt to provide warning, but the assassins had already swarmed her.

Though her Status had been weakened, the Level-6 adventurer refused to yield. Try as she might, however, as curse after curse and spell after spell hit her, her strikes turned sluggish. And the assassins took full advantage of it, using their curses and numbers to go in for the kill.

"You...damn...!!"

Assisted by the sacrifices of their comrades, they piled on more and more curses, using everything in their power to bring down their prey.

The man-made labyrinth and its party-dividing abilities were perfect for a combination tactic like this. They rushed her in a wave to overwhelm her, until finally, the Kukri knives were knocked from Tione's weakening hands.

"Gnngh!!"

Swords and fists rained down on her from all sides.

They hit her like a gale, their black robes whipping around her as they cut her to ribbons.

Her legs giving out, she fell to her knees, and one of the towering assassins raised his mace to deal the final blow.

"Miss Tione!!"

The sound of splattering flesh filled the passage.

"Tione! Tione!!"

Tiona slammed her fists into the orichalcum door again and again.

But there was no response. Not a sound. As the terror of being separated from her sister began to overtake her—

"Miss Tiona! Monsters! An—an army of them...!!"

"!"

She spun around at Elfie's frightened scream to find a new species of monster bearing down on them—the same water spiders Bete and his party had battled only a short while ago.

For a second, her thoughts froze, but she quickly overcame her hesitation with action. "Let's get outta here!"

"A-after you!"

The sheer number of spiders was enough to trample even her, to say nothing of Elfie and her other lower-level companions. Giving her sister, Cruz, and Olba a silent apology, she sprinted forward from the door, cutting a path through the monsters with her Urga and leading the others to safety.

Man, I don't have Finn, Gareth, Aiz, or Tione to help me now! Not even that good-for-nothin' Bete. Damn, this is getting bad! I'm not good at figuring this stuff out!

Intelligence and tact had never been Tiona's strong points, and they weren't helping her make heads or tails of the maze's myriad openings now, either. All she could do was run pell-mell down the path in front of her, worrying whether she could protect her lower-level peers desperately racing to keep up.

"—Gwaaugh!"

"Hey! Arcus?!" She spun around at the sudden scream from behind her to find one of her human companions on the ground, cradling his arm. It took her a second to realize what had happened, and her eyes widened at the sight of a monster latched onto him.

"Poison vermis?!"

Even second-tier adventurers feared the toxicity of the poison vermis. *Loki Familia* had suffered their fair share, as well, on the way back from their previous expedition.

"Elfie! Cynthia! Outta the way!" she shouted, not letting her surprise impede her attack. She swung her oversize Urga with swiftness and precision, slicing the vermis on Arcus's arm without so much as grazing his skin.

"It's too late...Without an antivenin, he's done for!"

"But why would poison vermis be in a place like this…?!"

Elfie and Cynthia ran to his side, cries of dismay on their lips. Poison vermis toxin was powerful enough to defeat even the strongest of status resistances, and the reality that they had nothing in their inventory to heal him set Tiona's thoughts whirling—when suddenly—

Another poison vermis tumbled toward her feet.

"…"

Her expression hardening, she slowly raised her gaze—and came face-to-face with the innumerable holes of the ceiling overhead, each one of them teeming with monsters.

"*Run!!*" she screamed.

They were off in a flash, while poison vermis dropped from the sky like acid rain the moment their feet left the ground.

"This is insane, this is insane, *this is insane!!*"

She dashed down the passageway with everything she had, supporting her poisoned comrade's shoulder. Purple bodies cascaded from the ceiling in an endless flow, secreting venom from their skin. Tiona's panicked chatter only served to spur on her companions; the footsteps of the two mages beat out a maddened tattoo on the ground below.

"Outrunning a dragon would be easier than this!!"

Their full-out sprint paid off, and they somehow managed to outrun the vermis waterfall.

But the unforgiving labyrinth wasn't about to let them rest just yet—

A heartbreaking *THUD!!* resounded in their ears.

"Another door?!"

"Miss Tiona! Behind us!!"

There wasn't even time to throw the new orichalcum door a dumbfounded glance. Spinning around, Tiona found yet another massive wave of poison vermis awaiting them.

It was a nightmarish scene: toxic maggots writhing on the floor, the walls, the ceiling, like an army of ants swarming their prey. It was enough to send nausea-induced goose bumps up their arms.

All at once, the poison vermis came at them.

"Okay, you nasty little—!!"

Tiona pushed Arcus toward the two mages and launched herself at the incoming mob, Urga flying. Its double blades flashed back and forth, creating a propeller-like barrier as it sliced through the charging maggots. Their tiny bodies were ripped to shreds one after another, pained squeals echoing off the walls.

Their escape route was gone. It was do or die at this point; Tiona barely had time to break a sweat.

All of a sudden, the poison vermis stopped in their tracks, their miniscule mouths opening.

"_____"

It was a single synchronized attack. And for a moment, Tiona felt time come to a halt around her.

In one concentrated stream, the toxic fluid shot straight for the adventurers.

"Gngh-*haw*!!"

Gareth's fist connected with the monster in his path, shattering its frame.

"Glad my ax helped Aiz escape, but I sure miss it now," the dwarven warrior grumbled to himself as he rent the beast limb from limb with his bare hands.

The room they currently occupied was teeming with water spiders. On high alert lest these unfamiliar foes catch them off guard, he and the rest of the group were fighting to keep the circle of monsters from closing in around them.

Dropped quite a ways. I'd dare say eight floors' worth, at least if we're counting with the Dungeon's middle floors.

He'd fallen through his fair share of pitfalls in the Dungeon's middle levels during his early days as an adventurer. Just recently, he'd taken a trip down The Dragon's Urn on the fifty-eighth floor during their previous expedition. By timing the fall, he was able to estimate their current location.

Lost damn near all my greenhorns, too...Could really use Tiona *and Tione right about now...*he thought, glancing worriedly in the direction of the followers still under his wing. Including Narfi, there were just three left, all of them second-tiers, and despite their valiant efforts against the monster swarm, they were growing visibly haggard.

"Mister Gareth! Enemy reinforcements!" Narfi cried out with a desperate flourish of her twin blades.

"!"

Gareth's eyes swept the room, only to find each of the countless exits suddenly brimming with drove after drove of black-robed Evils disciples.

"Stay away! Accordin' to Lefiya, that lot's willing to blow themselves up!"

Certainly, these Evils' Remnants seemed undaunted by death so long as it kept their Statuses—and their true names and affiliations with them—a secret, as they had learned during the fight in the pantry.

As if in response to Gareth's warning, the deviants before them now activated the Inferno Stones hidden beneath their robes.

"Atonement for this foolish desire!!"

"Gwwuuaaaaaaaaauuuuuuuuuuuuuugh?!"

The human bombs exploded within the wave of monsters, their cries combining with the pained screams of the beasts themselves.

"Run, all of ye!" Gareth shouted, and they were off in an instant, retreating from the onrush of blazing heat. They dove into the one passageway unoccupied by the black-robed apostles, momentarily throwing off their pursuers.

It didn't last, however, as their enemies were quick to follow. They came out of the woodwork like ants, one after another from the labyrinth's multitude of tunnels, and launched themselves at the group in fiery kamikaze attacks.

"I've heard the stories, but...this is worse than I ever imagined!" Narfi shrieked as she raced down the tunnels next to the dwarf.

"Aye, and in these cramped quarters, we've nowhere to run...!"

Gareth was forced to concede that they were in trouble, his features contorting in irritation.

They sped around an upcoming turn in the path—

—and the relentless onslaught behind them came to an abrupt halt.

"They...stopped?" Narfi asked in confusion, breath ragged.

Beside her, Gareth brought his hand to the wall, brows furrowing in suspicion. It was quiet now. The dogged footsteps and murderous hostility of their pursuers had been cut short, leaving the maze deathly still.

"—Lord Barca! Lord Thanatos! I've done it! Your loyal servant, Tris, has cornered the foul insurgents who'd dare to stand against us!"

The sudden shout from in front of them caused them to whirl around, only to find themselves face-to-face with a black-robed human who appeared every bit an Evils chieftain. Great salty tears poured from his eyes as his body trembled in what could have been either joy or fear, an altogether bizarre sight to behold.

As a jolt of fear rippled through the group, the man prepared to activate his stones.

—A suicide attack? From so far away?!

At this distance, the flames weren't likely to reach.

But perhaps more importantly, what had he meant by "cornered"? Trying to make heads or tails of the man's words, Gareth—

"_____"

—brushed his hands across an unfamiliar object, bringing him to examine it more closely.

There was something there, visible between the cracks of his fingers. A dazzling scarlet light radiating from the stone.

It was then that it hit him: Inferno Stones, the same as those hidden in the man's robes. And they'd been installed, evenly spaced, across the entirety of the walls both to their right and left.

"My Lord, I pray...pray that you grant me my heart's desire..."

The man self-destructed in a thunderous blast—

—setting off all the inlaid bombs in the walls, detonating the tunnel around them.

"Run!!"

They sprinted down the corridor as the heat and shock waves came at them. Like land mines beneath their feet, the Inferno Stones detonated one after another with successive roars that joined together in one mighty wave of pure flame rolling toward them as they ran.

It was a crematory trap. A desperate, wide-scale attempt to incinerate the intruders where they stood.

The stone covering the walls exploded, flying around them and revealing the adamantite beneath. Though the stout metal itself remained unscathed, the entirety of the tunnels it formed rose to a scorching temperature as the wild flames choked the air.

Beads of sweat slid down Gareth's and the group's temples as the massive conflagration lapped at their ankles.

Then, for the final blow.

A door came slamming down in front of them, blocking their path.

"!!"

Like an executioner's ax, it fell, just as it had with Tione and Tiona.

They whirled around to take the flames head-on, the blaze painting their faces a fierce vermillion—

"Ahhhhhhhhhhhhhhhhhhhhhhhhhhhhhhhhhhhhhhhhhhhhhhhhhhh!!"

With one final scream, they were swallowed by the inferno.

"There you are!"

As Bete and the rest of his group battled the monsters, a new contender appeared amid the pandemonium.

"...The hell is this guy?"

Clothed in an Evils robe, open at the front, he carried a long spear of deepest red, reminiscent of blood. While he was identifiably a human man, a dark hood that was as threadbare as the rest of his garments disguised the better part of his features.

"And what's up with those clothes?! You ain't foolin' anyone with that half-assed getup, dickhead!" Bete spat, turning away from the gaggle of monsters he was thrashing at the front of the group to face the newcomer head-on. Rakuta and the rest of the group were glancing back now, as well, even in the midst of their own fights.

The man himself—Dix—laughed, giving his spear a spin before resting it on his shoulder. He pointed in Bete's direction. "As much as I hate to leave a bad first impression—you've gotta die." He smirked, red eye narrowing behind the lenses of his goggles. "*Get lost in an endless nightmare!*"

In an instant, the spell was complete.

A short chant.

And ushering in with it, the nascent cries of a curse.

"*Phobetor Daedalus!!*"

The moment Bete's amber eyes caught sight of the ominous surge of red light coming for him, they widened with a snap.

"_____"

His next course of action was to run like hell.

Instinctive as it was for the battle-hungry werewolf to take the enemy head-on, even he understood that this was not the time. He didn't even issue an order to retreat, instead simply snagging Rakuta by her collar and hurling her down the nearest side tunnel.

A mere moment later, the passage they'd been occupying, along with their peers and the monsters they'd left behind, was awash in a wave of brilliant crimson light. And with it came a bloodcurdling, malicious echo that coiled around their very ears.

In the next instant:

"_____*Gngh!!*"

With a great roar, their companions, the monsters, everyone— *went berserk.*

"Wh—…Guys?!"

"…?!"

Swords, spears, fangs, and whips formed a flurry of haphazard attacks amid a spray of blood. Person, monster—it didn't matter who was who. Rakuta and Bete could only stare in shock at the inconceivable scene, friend attacking friend, monster attacking monster, all of them using anything they could lay their hands on to slaughter the being next to them.

"It's a curse…!" Bete hissed, one glance of the hysteria enough for him to realize it was too undignified to be proper magic. More specifically, it was a confusion curse, one that caused its victims to rampage blindly, attacking friend and foe alike until their strength gave out.

Quite the opening move from their new opponent—not only a short chant but a veritable killing blow, as well. Even Bete would have found himself prey to its effects had the side tunnel next to him not been so conveniently placed.

"I'm impressed, Vanargand…Most people wouldn't be able to dodge that attack after seeing it. Guess I should've expected more from *Loki Familia!*" Dix laughed gleefully in Bete's direction. Tapping his spear against his shoulder, he directed his gaze back toward the carnage, lips curling upward. All around him, weapon and claw continued to bite into flesh, staining the floor with human and monster blood. "You just gonna let this happen, wolf? If ya don't do somethin' soon, all yer little friends are gonna rip one another to shreds! Ha-ha…ha-ha-ha-ha-ha-ha-ha-ha-ha-ha-ha!!"

Bete could do nothing but scowl at the contempt.

Standing before his feast of blood and mayhem, the goggled man howled with laughter.

"Our ancestor…the master architect Daedalus…sought to create a masterpiece grander, more magnificent than even the Dungeon itself," Barca said as his eyes studied the pedestal. "And that monument is here…The man-made labyrinth: Knossos."

Images of *Loki Familia* flashed one after another in the watery film below him.

"To fulfill that wish…using the blueprints passed down to us generation after generation…is what we desire most in this world. We, his descendants, who share his blood, shall consummate his magnum opus, a work of genius *one thousand years* in the making."

As Tiona's group flashed across the surface, he narrowed his eyes, bringing one hand to the pedestal's large jewel. With a simultaneous flash of eye and jewel, he slammed down an orichalcum door in Tiona's path.

"Though it was with great reluctance that I installed this peculiar technology, beyond the scope of my ancestor's design…it was in the Evils' contract. And without their help, our dream will never reach fruition." The mechanism in the pedestal allowed him free control of the maze's doors from afar.

The technology was inoperable by all but those with the letter *D* emblazoned on their eye—descendants of Daedalus himself, like Barca. Using that technology now, he watched as Tiona and the rest of her group faced off against the vermis's mass poison attack.

"A malice far greater than that of a certain other Dungeon emanates from these walls. This is no mere fortress for sheltering the wickedness of Orario…No. The very moment you stepped foot within these halls, your fate was sealed…*Loki Familia*," he finished, eyes never leaving the pedestal. "Draw them away from their herd… Yes, one of the most basic axioms of the hunt. Adventurers are ever so weak without their parties to rely upon. And *Loki Familia* is no exception."

They would divide, and then they would conquer. Everything was going according to plan. Already, they were closing in—the assassins, the monster swarms, Valletta and the other Evils—driving each of the disunited *Loki Familia* parties into their own little corners.

"Even they are nothing without one another."

Again and again, the scene changed: to Finn, still barely conscious in Raul's arms; to Tione; to Tiona; to Gareth; to Bete, and each one of them was on the verge of being swallowed by the labyrinth's carefully laid traps.

Loki Familia had finally met its match.

Difficult as it was to believe, the truth was undeniable.

And it came in the form of a man-made labyrinth, hostile as even the Dungeon's depths.

"Without a key, you've no hope of storming the mighty keep of Knossos...Your time is up, *Loki Familia*," Barca finished coldly, eyes unfeeling as they watched the adventurers' features contort in burgeoning horror. "All that's left, then, are the elven pair...and the Sword Princess."

The scene in the water switched, finally, to the ones in question.

To the two elves...and to the golden-haired, golden-eyed swordswoman, hurrying like the wind.

"Lefiya! I will take the lead. Stay behind me!"

"U-understood!"

Lefiya acknowledged Filvis with a furious nod as she propelled herself forward.

They'd yet to discover any sort of clue as to their current location in the maze. All they could do was run in an effort to rejoin their separated companions and find a solution to this labyrinthine madness.

"...All clear. This way!"

Filvis was a magic swordswoman, so it was only natural that she would take the point position while a purely rearguard mage like Lefiya would stay to the rear. Peering around the upcoming corner to check for signs of enemies, she signaled for Lefiya to follow, and the two of them continued down the path.

"Lefiya...I think it would be best to search for the exit."

"Huh?"

"While I understand your desire to pursue your fallen comrades, finding a way out and soliciting help seems the wisest path."

Lefiya found herself at a loss for words.

She knew Filvis was right. Certainly, enlisting the help of Riveria and the others waiting outside would prove more productive than simply wandering aimlessly about the maze, which meant they'd need to alter their course: not down, in the direction Finn and the others had fallen, but up.

The logic was sound. And yet, somehow, Lefiya was finding it hard to agree.

They'll...be all right, surely? she told herself, unable to shake her worry.

Praying for the other party to be unharmed—and that, if they were, they'd reconvene shortly—she was jolted from her thoughts as the elf in front of her came to an abrupt halt.

Sticking out an arm to grab her, Filvis pulled her into the shadows of a nearby side tunnel.

"Wh-what is it?"

"Quiet." Filvis offered only one word in response.

Lefiya held her breath at the sharp tone of her voice, and soon, a figure appeared at the intersection in front of them.

...! That's...?!

Her eyes fell on a bluish-purple robe.

The figure was none other than the masked entity she'd first encountered in the twenty-fourth-floor pantry. All but completely concealed beneath a robe and silver gloves, it was a creature capable of manipulating the violas, at least according to reports from Finn and the others.

Just one...?

As far as they could tell, the masked creature was alone. As they watched to see which direction it would head, their target suddenly whirled around.

"...!"

Filvis pulled her arm in just in time for her to hide.

Their cover hadn't been blown. Probably.

Lefiya's heart was beating so loudly, she could feel its frenzied pulse all throughout her body. Filvis, too, was silent as the grave, her jaw tight.

They would be helpless if the creature were to summon its monster allies there. Holding their breath, they waited as the hooded figure stared in their direction—before abruptly turning on its heel at the sound of something farther down the passage.

It dashed off without a word.

"...It's gone..."

"Then we're safe for now...though that sounded like another one of those doors opening."

They'd become all too familiar with it while traversing the labyrinth—the distinctive sound of those impenetrable orichalcum doors opening and closing.

As Lefiya's slender elven ears twitched in response, Filvis nodded her agreement. Darting out from the shadow of their tunnel, they made for the masked creature. They were careful to keep their distance, putting just enough space between them to keep the figure in their sights without being seen. Turning corner after corner, even ascending a staircase, they finally stopped a short distance from what appeared to be an exit.

Standing in front of the recently opened door was a trio of hooded figures—their guide and two others.

Who are they...? Lefiya's mind raced as she peeked around the corner. The two new figures appeared to be talking, and from what she could make out of the shapes beneath their robes, one of them was male, while the other was female. Her eyes narrowed. *Is that a...god?*

Even from their current distance, she could just make out the undeniable sense of divine will emanating from one of the speakers. She watched as their masked friend led the two newcomers toward another door, opening it with a key before guiding them inside.

"Where does that lead, I wonder...?"

"That I can't say...but what I can say is that we've accomplished our goal. Look there—it leads outside," Filvis replied. Both elves glanced at the door their enemies had taken before directing their gazes at the unobstructed path that would point to their freedom. Whether the door had some kind of automatic shutoff function, they weren't sure, but for now, at least, it remained open. A quick peek outside rewarded them with the familiar sight of the hidden path that had first brought them into the maze.

No doubt, this would lead them straight to Riveria and the others.

"No enemies or monsters in sight, either. Let's go, then!" The relief was tangible in Filvis's voice.

Lefiya, however, hesitated.

"..."

"...Lefiya?"

Filvis turned around, bewildered, only for Lefiya to summon a magic circle without warning.

"*I beseech the name of Wishe!*"

"What are you—?"

She was casting her summon burst, Elf Ring.

In only a matter of seconds, she'd woven her spell as Filvis looked on in shock beside her.

"*Blow with the power of the third harsh winter, advent of the end— my name is Alf!*" she finished, transitioning into the final words of Riveria Ljos Alf's ice spell. As brilliant jade-colored light radiated from the magic circle, she gripped her staff in both hands before thrusting it forward. "*WYNN FIMBULVETR!*"

Three chilling spirals of ice and snow barreled toward the exit. Like a blizzard, they froze the path, including the open door, and turned the tunnel into a veritable ice cavern.

"This way..."

Yes. This way.

This way, even if their enemy was to use that key of theirs, that door wasn't going anywhere—at least for a while.

"...You go. Fetch Lady Riveria and the others and tell them what happened. I'm...going back!"

"Y-you can't be serious!" Filvis's voice cracked. Her features twisted in worry—before suddenly sharpening as she quickly scanned the perimeter. Voice low, she drew close, practically in Lefiya's face. "Going back? In this maze?! Are you trying to kill yourself?! What do you even expect to do on your own?!"

"I know what you are saying, and I agree…If I go back alone… I might accomplish nothing," Lefiya started, firm as she looked straight into Filvis's piercing scarlet eyes. "But if I just stand here and wait for help, it…it *might be too late!*"

"…!"

"I know where the exit is now, and this door will remain open at least a short while longer. If I go straight from here, I can greatly reduce the time it would take to find the others," she explained.

But Filvis refused to listen. "You're going to get yourself killed…" she nearly whispered, weakly shaking her head. Lefiya's plan was nothing more than naive, wishful thinking.

Filvis felt tears threaten to well up in her eyes. She needed her to stay.

But Lefiya would not be swayed.

Her mind had already been made up, as evidenced by the way she hoisted the cylindrical pack back onto her shoulders.

"I am sorry, Miss Filvis…but I simply cannot abandon my familia."

The words hit Filvis like knives.

Her eyes widening in surprise, she turned her gaze toward the floor, lip clenched between her teeth. For her, who had abandoned her companions during the Twenty-Seventh-Floor Nightmare, the words were too painful.

For Lefiya, however, Filvis's traumatic history was all the more reason for her to continue now. And Filvis understood Lefiya's resolve so well it hurt.

A heavy silence weighed down on the air around them, the seconds ticking away.

Finally, Filvis raised her head.

"…I'll come with you, then."

"What…? But…you need to go; you need to get hel—!"

"—I'm not going to leave you!!" she shouted.

Lefiya's shoulders gave a jump, and she held her breath for a moment.

"You…you think I can just leave a selfish, stubborn…wreck like you to fend for yourself?!"

"Miss Filvis…"

"Do you even care at all how I feel?…I can't…I can't let you die!"

"…!"

"I…I…" She attempted to turn her thoughts into words, but she was clearly struggling to hold in the rush of emotions.

Lefiya's chest squeezed painfully at the tremble in her crimson eyes. To think the other elf cared so deeply for her. It made her heart ache. And yet, she still couldn't take back her words.

Silently, she met Filvis's eyes with a woeful gaze of her own.

Finally, Filvis seemed to regain her composure. "…I will go with you, whether you choose to remain here or return to the maze. If you refuse to yield, then I shall do the same," she said, lips curled in a scowl.

It was enough to keep Lefiya from attempting to dissuade her.

They were too similar, Lefiya and Filvis. Like mirror images.

A wry smile crossed her face. Lefiya knew there would be no changing her mind. It was her own selfishness that had gotten Filvis tangled up in this mess in the first place.

"…"

She glanced at the frozen wall next to her. Great as the magic had been that had glazed it over, it was already starting to melt. Her eyes followed the length of the wall and the magic-resistant drop items that formed its canvas.

I'll simply have to believe…that Lady Riveria will know what to do. Somehow…

Moving just inside the hidden passageway, she placed her staff, Forest Teardrop, next to the wall. Before leaving, she cracked the magic jewel affixed to its point, waiting for the release of its azure-tinted magic essence, then turned back toward the maze and its halls of dim shadow.

"Let's go."

Filvis nodded wordlessly, then the two of them were off, back into the man-made labyrinth.

"Thank you…Miss Filvis."

"…"

There was no reply from the back in front of her.

Aiz's feet hit the ground as she ran.

Both for the friends who had fallen down in that trap and for a clue as to how she could save them.

"Just how long have they been building this place…?"

It was simply too enormous to have popped up overnight.

And the farther she progressed, the more obvious this became.

It was vast to the point of meaninglessness. The sheer complexity of its construction was on par with the Dungeon itself. She'd passed so many forks at this point that she'd lost her sense of direction entirely.

They'd truly underestimated the power of this place.

They had always thought that except for Levis and the other creatures, the Evils' Remnants were at a far lower level than them.

But as Aiz felt the insufferable chill of the labyrinth now, she knew they were anything but.

As worried as I am about Tiona and the others…I need to keep my sights on the enemy!

One particular enemy, in fact: the door-controlling Barca. Unfortunately, considering she had absolutely no idea where he'd gone, she had no choice but to comb the maze's passages one by one.

At the same time, she found it hard to believe that Barca was the only one capable of moving freely through the labyrinth. Which meant there must have been some sort of key—much like whatever the masked figure had used to open the door for them upon first entering the maze.

Aiz honed her first-tier-adventurer's senses, seeking out any sign of human life as she sped along, expeditiously cutting down any monsters that came across her path.

A staircase…!

Four of them, to be exact.

Strangely enough, her current floor seemed completely devoid of human presence. Piles of ash lay strewn about—the decayed corpses of monsters—and the walls and tunnels were a mess, giving her the feeling the entire area had been abandoned.

Still sensing nothing and fully prepared to race down the stairs and into the descending corridor far below—

"_____!"

She stopped.

Before her feet touched the steps.

Because her golden eyes had landed on a single side passage.

There was nothing off about it. Nothing different from the rest of the tunnels she'd traversed already. In fact, it seemed altogether like simply another dark passageway.

And yet, for some reason, she found herself unable to look away.

Almost as if it were drawing her in.

This feeling...

BA-DUMP. Her heart gave a leap in her chest.

The blood of her ancestor urged her forward.

"Gngh..."

Hesitation tugged at the back of her mind, and she glanced again at the staircase she'd been about to descend.

But all the same, her feet turned toward this new path.

Not a single magic-stone lantern lit the way; the tunnel was shrouded in darkness, and the farther she continued, the faster her heart accelerated.

She could see a faint light deep, deep within the shadow—an exit, perhaps, calling to her.

The door is...open...

She stepped out from the long tunnel into an open room—

"_____"

—and into another world, completely unlike the rest of the laby-rinth and its stony walls.

Thousands of pipes crawled across the floor's surface. They spanned the entire length of the circular room, and all of them were connected to large-scale tanks set into the room's walls. It was eerily reminiscent of a mage's studio. No, a lab room of sorts. And like the halls outside, it was covered in dust and ash, as though it had been out of use for some time and was now nothing but an abandoned relic. Only the colossal magic stone hanging from the ceiling in the center of the room still lived, giving off a phosphorescent glow that bathed the space in pallid blue.

"What…is this place?"

There were seven tanks in total, sitting around the circumference of the room. They were large enough to house a curled-up adult human, but the glass had long since cracked. Needless to say, they currently lay empty save for a greenish fluid stagnant on the floor and giving off a rancid odor.

Aiz reached toward the nearest vessel.

BA-DUMP.

Her blood churned.

Before she knew it, the world was spinning, just as it had back in Rivira, and she was overcome with a feeling of nausea.

She could feel it—the vestiges of a twisted spirit.

She was certain.

This vessel had once housed a crystal orb fetus.

"Then this room…"

—Was a facility for growing and preserving crystal orb fetuses that had been transported to the surface.

Did that mean there were seven fetuses? The same as the number of shattered tanks?

A chill ran down her spine.

Demi-spirits.

The same creature she and the rest of *Loki Familia* had finally faced off against down on the fifty-ninth floor—and seven of them were already on the surface.

Her breath caught in her throat, and she glanced around the derelict room.

"—So you *are* here."

All of a sudden, a woman's voice accosted her.

She whirled around in the direction of the newcomer.

"You...!"

"Enyo said you would come, drawn by the presence here like a moth to a flame. Good thing I didn't listen to those surface dwellers." The red-haired woman, Levis, entered the room via a separate tunnel. The creature was practically her archrival at this point, and seeing her here now was enough to send a jolt of panic through Aiz's veins.

"It's been a while, Aria, since we last faced each other...Since the day I tasted agony because of you," she continued, the same cold, calculating voice as when they'd first met. Her green eyes burned with scarcely contained acrimony—a thirst for revenge that she planned on finally quenching. The blackened sword she carried glinted with a dull, foreboding sheen.

"The orbs...They were here, weren't they?"

"Must I answer that? Or are you really that blind?"

"Where are they now?"

"Hidden within the labyrinth. Perhaps you'd like to find out for yourself...if you can." A silent bloodlust implicitly warned Aiz that Levis had no intention of letting her do so.

It was an unbridled ferocity Aiz had never faced before. Prickles of anxiety gathering beneath her collar, she readied her Desperate for the upcoming fight...only to catch sight of something that made her stop.

"That blood...whose is it?" she asked, referring to the red fluid decorating Levis's sword. The presence of blood meant Levis had already faced off against someone else—another one of the intruders. Given the fact that *Loki Familia* were the only others present at the moment, it likely belonged to one of her companions.

The thought brought images to her mind of their faces, so far, far away.

She felt her chest clench.

"Oh, this...?" Levis replied, glancing down at her sword. "That prum's. The one with the spear."

Time slowed to a halt.

"Though I wasn't able to finish the job, those Evils clods are surely doing so as we speak."

"That—that's not possible!"

"I assure you, it is."

"Finn would never lose!!" she screamed at a volume normally unthinkable for her.

As Aiz fought to regain her composure, Levis reached dispassionately toward her belt, tossing something at Aiz's feet.

"_____"

Clink! The golden spearhead clattered as it fell.

It was Finn's Fortia Spear, cleaved from its shaft.

Everything around her sounded like it was going farther and farther away.

"There's no need to fear, though. Once I deal with you...the rest of your friends are next on my list."

The words hit her ears like a dissonant chord.

In that one second, her thoughts became clear.

"Gnngh!!"

Using a pipe as leverage, she threw herself forward to become a raging wind.

She saw nothing but red as she shrieked through the air, sword flying at Levis.

"You? Attacking me first? This is certainly new," Levis noted calmly as Aiz came at her with everything she had—

—before being batted away.

"?!"

The impact rippled through her arms, and shock colored her features as she immediately prepared herself for the next attack.

But Levis blocked it just as effortlessly as the first. One after the next, she deflected each of the Sword Princess's patented strikes with undiluted power and speed.

In fact, the dance of swords was so fervent that Levis's sword gave a sudden *crack!* as a chipped piece flew through the air.

"...Aha, I see," she mused, glancing down at her sword as if she had realized something before stepping back from the reckless rain of blows.

But despite the damage to Levis's weapon, it was Aiz's heart that was beating out of control and Aiz's hands that prickled with a numbing pain. The Levis she was fighting now was on a completely different level from the one she'd faced on the twenty-fourth floor.

"That was close. I'll simply have to kill you with this." Levis ignored Aiz's tremors as she tossed aside the broken sword and drew a second longsword from her belt instead. "Your wind, Aria. I want to see it."

In that instant, the aura around Levis changed.

"I wouldn't want you dying too quickly on me."

She leaped, splitting the ground beneath her.

"——Hngh?!"

It was too fast, invisible almost, and Aiz's pupils dilated in disbelief.

Then came the impact and, with it, a roar that shook the entirety of the room. The sword she'd raised in defense was nearly flung from her hands.

Levis didn't stop there, her next strike hitting before Aiz even had a chance to find her footing. And though she managed to parry just in time thanks to her skill, the crazed dance kept her confined to one place.

The attacks came at her in a blur, sending locks of her golden hair flying; the ground, the pipes, everything crashed and tumbled around her as the glass of the tanks shattered beneath the frenzied blade.

Aiz could barely think, let alone plan out any sort of strategy as the room around her transformed into a scene of utter carnage.

"*Awaken, Tempest!!*" she cried out, activating her wind enchantment, Airiel. She leaped at the creature, armor of wind engulfing her body and honing her sword.

Only.

"You humans. So affected by the death of your companions."

Levis's speed simply rose to meet hers.

It seemed that even before Aiz's armor of wind, she was no longer worried that one full-powered hit could very well end her life.

"Your emotions betray you."

"_____"

Her attacks came at carefully timed intervals now to slip between the gaps of the raging gale dominating Aiz's field of vision.

With one well-placed strike, she sent Aiz's sword flying.

Her wind was reduced to feeble shreds, leaving her with no defense.

Levis seized the opening, directing one powerful downward strike toward the defenseless Sword Princess.

"I win, Aria."

Cutting through what remained of her armor of wind, the sword carved a diagonal crimson slash in the air.

"Ah——"

It was a direct hit, plunging through her breastplate in a cascade of blood.

Like fire, the searing pain overtook her body as Levis's killing blow struck home.

CHAPTER
4

The SWORD'S Wind CALLS

Гэта казка іншага сям'і

З меча прыйшоў да яго, як

From within the gloom, the watery film glimmered, hazy atop its pedestal.

Gazing down at it, fixated on the reflected images, was the ever-impassive Barca.

"The Sword Princess, too, has fallen, at Levis's hand...Our victory is but a matter of time..."

He muttered to himself, watching as the golden-haired, golden-eyed swordswoman tumbled to the floor in a pool of blood after the red-haired creature's critical hit. Her plight in the tank room wasn't the only scene playing out on the watery screen—the rest of *Loki Familia* were also shown in similarly dire straits.

Barca watched everything from his window into Knossos. "All that remains are those two elves...whose location currently eludes me..." he said slowly. The tiniest of creases appeared between his normally expressionless brows.

He had lost sight of the two elves.

Somehow, no doubt unintentionally, they were moving into his blind spots—just out of sight of the statues and reliefs that housed his all-seeing "eyes" in the labyrinth. Without knowledge of their exact location, operating doors or setting off traps was meaningless.

As if on cue, they appeared on the screen, finally having stepped foot in front of an eye. However—

"More magic...?"

His view disappeared in an instant as the white elf unleashed a tendril of lightning.

They were destroying them—the statues and reliefs. Not on purpose, but simply during the course of fighting the monsters they encountered in the tunnels. The Thousand Elf's spells were especially devastating, taking out whole pieces of stonework in one brilliant flash of her magic.

It seems they were momentarily back on the first floor...but now they've descended again to the fourth. Their movements are...irregular. What are they aiming for? he mused, prioritizing the chance glances he received of their progress through the maze among his surveillance. It was in this attempt to anticipate their target that he realized something with a start.

"If they remain on this path, they'll..."

"There, Lefiya!"

"*ARCS RAY!!*" Lefiya cried out before unleashing her magic in the direction indicated.

Instantly, the gleam of light filled the tunnel, disintegrating the legion of assembled water spiders and, with it, the surrounding stone face.

It had already been some hours since they'd discovered the exit up on the first floor, and currently, they were progressing through the deeper tunnels, taking out any monsters they encountered.

Though the rampant use of magic was quickly draining Lefiya's Mind, for better or for worse, they'd yet to come across any Evils associates during their trek to the fourth floor. They also made sure to keep track of their movements, marking the walls with white chalk to designate their way back.

"!"

"Miss Filvis?"

The change was sudden.

Lefiya came to a screeching halt when she saw Filvis's shoulders jump, and her eyes followed the other elf's line of sight.

She found herself face-to-face with an unusual change in scenery—a monstrously sized corridor, unbefitting an underground labyrinth. Blue magic-stone lanterns lined the walls, offering their ethereal refulgence in place of the sun's light, and rows of perfectly aligned columns stretched to the ceiling.

It looked almost like a ruin of some sort, or at least that was the first thought to pop into Lefiya's mind, thanks to the large drawing covering one of the corridor's walls.

"A mural...?" Lefiya murmured in awe.

And, indeed, it was.

In fact, there were many of them, some drawn on the red stone, others etched into the cracked and faded rock face...all of them, no doubt, lifted from various ruins outside the city and pasted here on the labyrinth's walls.

And all of them depicted similar ideas: panic and hysteria as humans escaped from colossal dragons, ominous birds, and other egregious types of monsters. One could practically hear the frightened screams, the bestial cries echoing from the images.

Calamity and chaos. A feast of destruction and clamoring.

As Lefiya stood there in that room of disquiet, she felt a sense of revulsion wash over her.

What in the world was this place? As her brain searched for answers, her azure eyes took in the sights until they stopped on another of the murals.

"Is this...a dragon?"

It was different from the rest.

At its center was a dragon of elephantine proportions, and surrounding it was a sextet of young maidens. At first glance, they appeared to be praying, eyes closed and hands clasped.

"Sacrificial maidens, perhaps?...Or some sort of holy saints?"

There were references to such practices in the Ancient Times of a thousand years past—rituals on the frontier lands, in which young girls had been sacrificed to monsters ascended from the Dungeon in hopes of appeasing their wrath.

The cracked, decayed image was pulling her in.

"And that dragon...it's—"

Lefiya was gazing into the image as if in a trance, when suddenly.

"Nidhogg...is the name you're looking for."

The funereal voice slithered out from the encompassing gloom.

"?!"

It belonged to neither her nor Filvis, and the shock that someone else was in the room with them sent Lefiya whirling around.

A god stepped from the shadow of a nearby pillar.

"Behemoth, Leviathan, the One-Eyed Dragon...the marks of the Three Great Quests. But before these black dragons terrorized the land, there was another: a grisly creature that plunged the surface into the depths of fear and despair."

"Wh-who are you?!"

Long hair like a woman's cascaded down his back. And his features seemed to be molded from the shadow itself. The air surrounding him reeked of noxious decadence. Though he boasted the graceful refinement characteristic of the gods, Lefiya could not recall meeting another god quite so despondent.

"I am called Thanatos...guardian deity to the dregs of the group you call the Evils."

"!"

Lefiya's breath left her, and she quickly readied her spare wand. "Then, you're the one carrying on the Evils' dying wish...?!"

"Though, honestly, it's more a simple gathering of those the Guild once deemed 'evil'...Those of us who are left, that is," the god continued with a laugh. "At any rate, I won't deny I 'lead' them in a way. True, I picked up dear Valletta and the rest of her crew, bereaved as they were after their guardian deity was finished off, and certainly I've been accumulating a number of children these past five years... Why, I'm even the one who decided to accept their invitation to join them in their evil plans and lay waste to Orario. It was aaaaall me."

He really was the last one—the only "evil" god who'd escaped being repatriated to Heaven.

Assimilation, solicitation, reorganization, and finally, expansion of power: that was how the remaining Evils associates had reached their current level of authority, and hearing this new god say so sent Lefiya reeling from shock.

The only way to describe Thanatos was as a vast, bottomless abyss of impenetrable darkness.

Lefiya swallowed hard, staring down the god in front of her before slowly forming her next words. "Are you...Enyo?"

She'd once heard Levis use the name of this preeminent being.

Even the name itself, Enyo, meant "Destroyer of Cities." And the rest of her familia had come to believe this entity was the puppet master pulling all the strings.

"Me? Enyo?...Ha-ha...ha-ha-ha-ha-ha, oh, my dear, you've got it all wrong!" Thanatos denied with an amused laugh.

It was an answer Lefiya hadn't been expecting, and one that made her glance this way and that in confusion. She and Filvis found themselves at a loss as the deity in front of them continued to chuckle.

"I've never even seen or heard of Enyo. I'd be hard-pressed to provide evidence that such a god even exists!...God? Mortal? Who knows. But most definitely not me."

"You...you've never seen or heard...?"

Their confusion compounded on itself.

Wasn't Enyo the one commanding the Evils? Utilizing the power of the creatures belowground? How could Thanatos, currently allied with Levis and the Evils, not know the true form of this "Enyo" entity?

Truly, this mysterious name was becoming the cause of sheer confusion.

"That I haven't. What I do know, however, is that Enyo is the mastermind behind our current plot of calamity and intrigue, at least according to my dear Levis and our masked friend. That, and the one who brought in all these murals from some ruin or another," he responded with a shrug, glancing at the dragon-and-maiden-adorned wall nearby. "Nidhogg is a symbol of darkness and despair...and what Enyo wants to eventually become, if I'm to understand correctly."

What Levis and her friends were supporting wasn't just a destroyer of cities but the destroyer of Orario. If Orario were laid to waste, it would be open season on the rest of the lower world; monsters would be free to wreak havoc and destruction as they pleased. And with the added threat of the Corrupted Spirit, eclipsing the world in shadow and despair was very plausible.

A shiver ran down Lefiya's spine.

"But let's talk about something cheerier, shall we? For instance, your having made it this far. A surprise, really. Two souls, undeterred by Knossos's tangled halls. What were your names again? Let's see now..." Thanatos mused, appearing to rack his brain. He seemed honestly impressed at what, to them, had simply been luck. "You're...dear Lefiya, the one called Thousand Elf, yes. And you're..." His deep-purple eyes moved from Lefiya to Filvis. "...Maenad. Filvis, as I recall...Though this is strange. Has *Loki Familia* taken on a stray?"

He cocked his head at this, clearly confused as to how Filvis had ended up here.

"...Ah, yes. That's right." His confusion morphed into a smirk. His lips curling upward in a shape reminiscent of the reaper's scythe, he fervently nodded. "You, too, met with a terrible fate...during the Twenty-Seventh-Floor Nightmare."

"!"

Filvis's shoulders gave a sudden tremble. As her scarlet eyes widened, she was left speechless.

"Miss Filvis!"

"Let me just put this out there now, but...I had nothing to do with that, I assure you."

Lefiya quickly stepped in front of Filvis, one of the few survivors, protecting her from Thanatos's ridicule.

"Why?! Why would you want to lay Orario to ruin?! You're a god, aren't you?! Why would you want to wreak havoc across the mortal realm?!" she shouted, voice ragged. It was a question not only to him but to the rest of the "evil" gods.

"Erm, well...we all have our reasons, I suppose. Even among us 'evil' gods, our motivations have varied," Thanatos answered, his earlier smile still playing on his lips. "Some are simply bored; others wield a natural distaste for order; still others are nothing but necessary evils for the heroes of this world to overcome...While it's true that some wouldn't even apologize for the suffering they've wrought, we're not all the epicurean sadists you seem to think we are."

"...!"

He'd read her like a book. Even now, Lefiya's thoughts had gone straight to her confrontation with Kali in Meren—the hedonistic Goddess of War who sought nothing but pleasure and the excitement of the unknown in the mortal realm.

"As for my motivations, well...I'm the God of Death," Thanatos confessed with another scythe-like smile. He was the ruler of mortality itself. "Isn't it only natural for death to desire as many lives as possible?"

"‼"

A chill ran through Lefiya's body. Next to her, Filvis felt the same, her breath catching in her throat. In that single moment, they felt as though they'd touched the god's madness. A place where there was no reason, no pretext, not even emotion or principles. And somehow, though they'd never deign to admit it, within that vortex was an echo of divine providence and truth.

As Lefiya stood overwhelmed, Thanatos raised his hands with a laugh. "I kid! I kid! Honestly, up in Heaven, I did my job, as diligent as they come. Workaholic, actually...Managing you kids' souls as they ascended to Heaven, giving them a thorough bleaching, then sending 'em right back so they can start again as someone new."

"...Then you're in charge of...reincarnating the denizens of this world?"

"Exactly. I gave those old, worn-out souls a new outlook on life. They're as pure and clean as newborn babes when they leave me. It was pretty fun, actually," he explained, glancing idly at the ceiling as Lefiya's lips parted in awe. There was a hint of nostalgia in his eyes, mixed with traces of ecstasy. "I miss the good ol' days. Souls came in one after another...I did my work..."

"..."

"But it's different now. Orario's changed things. It sealed the monsters...and even the Dungeon itself."

Lefiya quickly realized Thanatos was referring to the Ancient

Times, back when monsters made their way freely to the surface, slaughtering human and demi-human alike. It was an age of iterative cycles of fear and war that sealed the fates of both humanity and beast.

"Truthfully, I know that wasn't right…I know those things shouldn't have been crossing their borders and creating havoc up on the surface as they did, but that doesn't mean I can't miss it."

"What…?"

"The lower world's teeming with life, now that they've received the thoughtless gift of the Falna. Life and death are two sides of the same coin, you see? Without souls ascending to Heaven, the cycle, well, stops. Which is why I developed a new little outlook on life myself…"

At this, Thanatos gestured with his index finger and thumb, letting out a brief chuckle.

"It would be all right if just a *few more* of the children die."

The feeling that struck them was electric.

A thrill of horror, like the deepest of despairs.

This wasn't an "evil" god, intent on the destruction of order, and neither was this a seeker of the unknown, committing crimes of schadenfreude.

No, this was a god with a sense of moral obligation, who felt it was his duty to correct the world in the only way he knew how: rampant death. He, himself, had said he was nothing but diligent, earnest, loyal, and fair—a description that contained no lies. The concepts of "good" and "evil" meant nothing to him.

No, the only concept he understood was nihilism.

He truly epitomized death itself.

"…Then…your followers are…" Filvis started slowly, as though just having realized something.

Thanatos nodded, his eyes narrowing. "Exactly. I offer my children a path after death."

"Wh-what does that even mean…?"

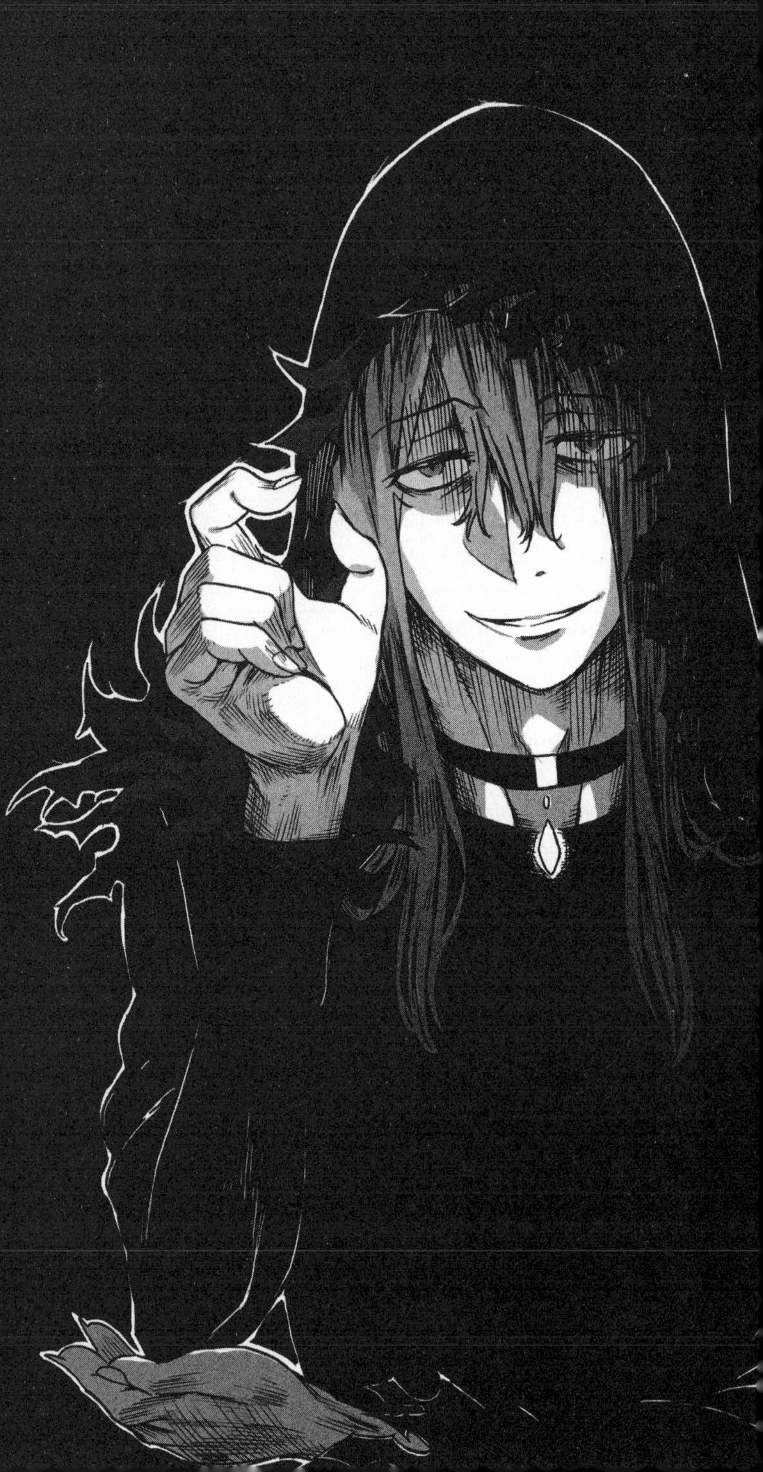

"Think, Lefiya dear. All those Evils bumpkins down in the twenty-fourth-floor pantry? Who sacrificed their own lives and blew themselves to smithereens? Why on earth would they be so unhesitating, I wonder...?"

Lefiya gasped. "You promised them passage to the next life...?"

"That I did. One by one, I forge their contracts. One by one, they sacrifice themselves to my will. Then...once Orario's been destroyed...and once I've returned to Heaven...I'll restore their lives, as well as those of any loved ones they've lost to death."

For those who'd lost someone precious, when they were overcome with grief at the loss of a family member, friend, lover, or partner, it was nothing short of the deal of a lifetime.

For Thanatos, however, they were easy pickings.

With sweet words, he lured them in.

He enticed them with the thought of being reunited with their loved ones in the next life.

"How...how could you do such a thing...?!"

That was who they were fighting, the true identity of Thanatos's army of the dead—ordinary humans, bereft of their beloved, who'd forged a contract with the devil in hopes of reuniting with their loved ones in the next life. For the members of *Thanatos Familia*, death was a door to their dearest companions and the reason they so readily gave their lives.

This was how the Evils had been able to mobilize so many so quickly even after their previous defeat. The world was rife with the misery of death, which made Thanatos indispensable for their recruitment purposes.

His followers were nothing more than puppets of the God of Death, freely sacrificing their lives for a second chance.

"You think you can just do whatever you please with human life? These are our lives! Even if your followers are reincarnated, they won't have any memory of their pasts...!" Lefiya shouted in accusation, unable to tolerate the way he toyed with people's grief.

"And that's exactly what I tell them, along with the rest of the rules, but none of them seem bothered in the least. They all tell me the opportunity to see someone so precious again outweighs the memory loss that comes with it," Thanatos replied simply. "Everything is their choice. I don't coerce them. There are even a few who believe they'll be different. That their love for their lost one is so strong, they will be the special exception that remembers, even if no one else ever does...Heh, the Goddess of Love might get a little chuckle from that."

As if he were reading the minds of his followers, Thanatos laughed in obvious mirth this time.

In scorn at their lack of enlightenment.

"But who am I to doubt them, hmm? Perhaps a miracle will occur...An Irregular unlike any before witnessed by us gods. So I never refute their delusions."

"You can't just shirk your responsibility in this whole mess!" Lefiya cried out.

"I'm not shirking anything. I wish for it just as much as they do, Lefiya dear...I have high expectations for the abilities of these... earthly children. It would certainly be nice if it came true, after all," Thanatos countered, not bothering to hide his genuine beliefs. "And they make for such moving tearjerkers, as well...which I must admit are my favorite kinds of stories."

Lefiya found something so aggravating about him, about the way he talked, the way he looked at her, the way shadow darkened his smile. It made her proud elven blood boil, almost as though he'd disgraced one of her own brethren.

The more her rage built, the more she wanted to beat the God of Death right where he stood. That was, until—

"Lord Thanatos!"

His reinforcements arrived before the elves could move.

"?!"

"Are you unharmed?!"

"I'm fine, I'm fine, truly...Though I must apologize to you, Lefiya dear, for keeping you here this dreadfully long time."

Lefiya bit her lip as she watched the black-robed followers of

Thanatos Familia rush into the room. There were enough of them that any action she took would prove futile.

The important question now was how they were going to get out of here.

"Lefiya. Close your eyes."

"Miss Filvis?"

The whispering voice came from behind her, just loud enough for her to hear.

Immediately following the command, Filvis pointed her wand at the ground.

"Purge, cleansing lightning—DIO THYRSOS!"

The short chant was complete in less than a second, summoning a golden bolt of lightning that detonated the ground.

"?!"

"Oh dear, that's awfully bright."

The entire group of robed figures, Thanatos included, brought their arms up instinctively to shield their eyes from the light.

"Now!!"

"Right behind you!!"

Taking advantage of the split-second opening, they ran.

"Damn elves! After them!"

Thanatos, meanwhile, simply laughed as he watched the robed throng give chase.

"What a fabulous little trick."

"Lord Thanatos!" those who remained with him for protection scolded. "You shouldn't be wandering about alone without an escort! Not with *Loki Familia* running amok throughout the labyrinth! If anything were to happen to you...!"

"My sincerest apologies. Had a little matter to attend to, was all... Though now that you mention it, how are things going?"

"...The majority of *Loki Familia* is now trapped on the eighth floor thanks to Lord Barca's plans. He has assured us it's only a matter of time before they're properly dealt with. Lady Valletta and her men have also subdued Braver, Vanargand, and the Sword Princess..."

one of his officers explained, knowing full well the advantage they currently held over their invaders.

"Marvelous. Then things are going swimmingly!" The ever-fickle Thanatos let out a guffaw. Just thinking about their impending victory was enough to widen his smile. "Does this mean we've won?" he mused, sending his gaze toward the steely walls of the fortress that protected them even now.

After a moment, he made to leave.

"—Things have taken quite the interesting twist, I see."

The voice came from behind him, prompting him to turn around. "You...?"

"Raul! Take the three on the right!"

"O-on it!"

Anakity severed the legs of the nearest water spider with her light-sword as Raul mowed through another set of the fiends with his short spear. With Valletta still hot on their trail, they were doing their best to fend off the incoming waves of these new species. Stopping wasn't an option, and they threw themselves down one empty passageway after the next as they obliterated any monsters that crossed their paths.

On and on they fled into the darkness down those tunnels, staying in a formation to protect the human girl carrying a scarcely breathing Finn.

"A dead end?!"

"Not another one...!"

Aki grimaced at the scream of warning from their scouts up ahead. Repelling an incoming monster with her left buckler, she returned it with a swipe of her sword, dismantling it in seconds. As it was the last one of the bunch, once it had been laid to rest, the attacks briefly stopped.

"Are you in here, Fiiiiiiinn?!"

"...?! Right! To the right!"

But then, Valletta's great voice boomed from behind them, and Raul yelped, leading the party down the one remaining path.

Running was their only option at this point. Even as the ragged breaths of his companions revealed their fatigue, Raul could think of no better strategy to keep them alive.

"Raul, they're leading us right where they want us! Can't you see? We just keep going deeper and deeper into the maze!" Aki pointed out from next to him.

"...! Then...then why aren't they attacking us...?!"

"Probably trying to wear us down little by little..."

Raul's face paled at this.

It did not escape the notice of his second-tier cat companion. Calling out to the rest of the group, she issued a command in his stead: that they should look for an opening when no monsters or pursuers were nearby and stop for a moment to share what little potions and water they had left.

"Here you go, Captain..."

The human girl in charge of Finn spoke softly as she laid the prum out on the ground. For the moment, at least, magic had frozen his wounds—Aki had ordered the emergency measure to keep his injuries, still un-healable thanks to the curse, from bleeding out.

"...Hngh...nn..."

Finn's lips parted as if he was trying to say something, but he couldn't seem to form the words.

They'd never seen their captain like this before. His fragile state symbolized the hopelessness of their current predicament, lowering their morale all the more.

"If he doesn't get help soon, then he'll...We'll..."

No one knew who said it. But the unfinished words hung over them like the grim reaper's shadow.

With every encounter, their wounds increased and, with them, a building sense of relentless despair. The mental burden was even greater than the physical, and it was reaching its peak now that they were completely lost in the middle of this prisonlike labyrinth.

"Stop talking like that! Calm down and chin up! If we don't, we'll...we'll..." But not even Aki could keep her voice steady during her desperate attempt to lift their spirits.

Raul felt an inescapable sense of defeat wriggle through him like a demonic worm. Not even Aki, already superior to him and attempting to do his job for him, would last much longer. If somebody didn't hold her back, that slender body of hers was simply going to break.

—*This is it.*

—*This is the end.*

For me. For Aki. For everyone.

All of us. We're all about to die; that demoness's laughter will swallow us whole—.

"...ul."

But right as these thoughts had reared up in his mind.

Just as he was about to hang his head in defeat, the tiniest, faintest sliver of a voice reached his ear.

"...Ra...ul..."

From the prum, nearer to death than any one of them.

Finn's nearly inaudible appeal pricked at his ear.

"———ngh!!"

Raul's eyes popped open with a start.

In the claustrophobic tomb that was to become their final resting place, his captain had provided the light he needed to see the way. Heart nearly thumping out of his chest, Raul felt the strength return to his fists.

We can't give up...not without a fight!!

With one proverbial punch from his tightly clenched hands, he sent his despair-ridden heart sailing into the darkness.

How can I sit here and do nothing?!

Who was it Finn had entrusted the party's safety to? Who was it Aki had always been there to support?

Right now, Raul's greatest fear was to betray the trust in Finn's blurred eyes looking up at him. How could he abandon his duty and lead into ruin the party his captain had counted on him to protect?

You need to pull yourself together, Raul Nord...!

That was what being a party was all about. That was what being a leader was all about.

Seeking one's worth through sheer adversity.

Why else would he have spent those many days tagging along behind his glorious leaders if not for this day? Why else would they have imparted to him their knowledge and guidance, if not for this day?

—Everything had led him to this very moment.

Yes, that was what he had to tell himself. That was what he had to convince himself of.

Fake it if you have to, Raul! You are the wolf. You are the wolf. Now...HOWL!!

Grinding his teeth together, he hurled his inhibitions to the wind.

"—Weeeeeeeeeeeee can do this, people!!"

It was a passionate, high-pitched squawk.

The comical timbre was so unbefitting to their situation that Aki's tail gave a startled jump, and the rest of the group stared at him with open mouths.

"Now...now is the time for action! We have to stay calm and—! And carefully assess the situation...!"

Tongue fumbling, shoulders shuddering, fists trembling, he screamed.

He was a pitiable sight that became even more so as he gave 110 percent...and as Aki and the rest of his companions simply stared at him, eyes glassy—they finally let out a collective sigh.

"...Huh? Wh-what gives, guys? What was that for...?!"

"...Somehow? Seeing you like that actually calmed me down," Aki explained, her disbelief melting into a smile.

"Yeah! I mean, you're pretty much the least dependable person ever, so it kinda makes us realize we have to get our shit together," someone else piped up as laughter and dry smiles rippled through the group.

The shadows of anguish and despair that had plagued their faces were gone.

All thanks to one of Raul's few merits.

They knew they had to man up, had to support one another, because Raul was a hopeless mess.

Somehow, albeit via a method far different from Finn's, Raul had managed to lift the party's spirits in a way only he could. It was a talent not even the first-tier greats possessed—not Finn, not Riveria, not Gareth, not Aiz. No, only him.

And seeing the smiles return to his companions' faces was enough to calm his own anxiety, as well.

"—This is an adventure, after all!"

And he didn't stop there.

"We've gotta give it everything we've got! Get your swords ready and let's do it! This is how the mettle of true adventurers is tested!— The captain would say the same thing!"

Raul might have been ordinary, but he wasn't a fool.

He'd amassed a great deal of experience, burning into his memory the backs of the familia elites as he studied their every move, every motion. And as he wove his speech now, the hearts of his peers stirred in response, and their heads nodded with resolve.

The light had returned to their eyes. They were *Loki Familia* once more.

Even Finn, watching them from afar, curled his bloodied lips upward in the faintest of smiles, his eyes crinkling.

"Let's put our heads together, guys! Those bastards still think they've got the advantage, which puts us in the perfect position to strike back!"

At Raul's urging, they set their minds to work, using what short time they had available to rattle off as many ideas as they could.

"We know that running around aimlessly will get us nowhere... The quickest solution, then, would be to simply steal that key of theirs."

"Yeah, but they've got way more manpower than we do. They wouldn't be chasing us in the first place if they were worried we could actually pull off a counterattack. Stealing that thing won't be easy."

"True…but we also can't let them keep pushing us farther into the maze. No matter what we do, we're gonna have to try to get past them."

Aki listened to the three opinions from her peers before speaking up herself. "I'm almost positive Valletta and her goons have something that keeps those new species from attacking them."

"Huh? Whaddaya mean by that?" Raul this time.

"Think about it—tamers and creatures are the only ones who can control those crazy colored monsters, right? So if these Evils psychopaths were to release monsters all over their hideout, they'd run the risk of being attacked themselves."

Raul and the others were quiet for a moment, then, as if on cue, their faces brightened in realization.

"So far, all we've seen down here are those water spiders…which means there must be some way to keep those things from attacking."

"And also that those spiders are basically an army built specifically to guard this place…"

"Exactly. Aside from that very first encounter, we haven't seen a single one of those violas."

Even then, the giant flower creatures had been lurking behind those orichalcum doors, meaning it was highly likely they were being kept separate from the rest of the maze and had been put there solely for use in that trap.

"Now, whether this is some sort of special trait of the new species, an odor, or even an item, we don't know…" Aki continued, her feline ears flicking back and forth as she surveyed their surroundings. "But whatever it is, it's making the enemy careless. So if we can use that to our advantage somehow and shake things up…"

It was a plan that made sense, to be sure, and Raul found himself unconsciously humming in affirmation, his hand going toward the pouch at his waist in search of anything that might give them an idea.

"…Ah."

The plan popped into his head when his hand came in contact with a certain item, an item he had considerable experience with from his expeditions in the Dungeon.

Color draining from his face, he drew it from his pouch. He wore several expressions until finally, after working up the nerve, he opened his mouth to relay his scheme.

"Y-you can't be serious! There's no way I'm letting you do that, Raul!"

"We don't have any time, Aki! We're past sitting back and leisurely talking this out!...I think," he countered, turning around even as the rest of the group voiced their own objections. He approached the one person who hadn't put in his own two cents—the prum lying on the ground.

"Captain...I need to use you for a little bit," he told him, face sallow.

Finn just smiled.

"Where *aaaaarrrreeee* you, Finn, my sweet?"

Valletta and the rest of her assassin troupe made their way down one of the maze's tunnels. They numbered ten in total—enough that they'd be able to take out Braver's little rescue party in one fell swoop.

"*Hiss...*"

A water spider appeared in front of them—before simply passing them by.

In fact, they crossed many of the brightly colored creatures, and all of them simply ignored the way the assassins readied for battle at the unfamiliar presences and continued along.

"Stop pissin' yourself at every monster, you pussies! So long as we've got this crystal, those vargs won't even come close," Valletta sneered, pulling out the small crystal she kept tied around her neck. It was just as Aki had hypothesized—the Evils *did* have something that kept the new species of monster at bay.

They were a new monster—vargs.

By harvesting crystals from a certain species of plant and carrying them with them at all times, the assassins could fool the spiders into thinking they were their own brethren. This allowed them to wander the labyrinth's passageways without fear of attack.

"Sure has gotten quiet, though. What are they up to, hmm? Hiding, perhaps? Or...has my favorite midget whispered some scheme to them from his deathbed, I wonder?" she mused with a crinkle of her brows. When she caught sight of something underfoot, however, she laughed. "Pfft, ha-ha! That sweet, sweet blood of yours will still show me the way!"

Crimson droplets of blood dotted the floor, like footprints leading her to her wounded prey. She licked her lips in anticipation.

...And oh, how they've grown, too! Not like those random splatters from before. He might as well be asking me to come kill him!

One after another, the bright-red specks called to her. A trap, perhaps? Her lips curled into an impish smile as her fellow assassins cautiously scanned the area. They'd slowed their pace now, prepared for an ambush, following the bread-crumb-like trail of blood until it led them to a large intersection where a multitude of different tunnels branched off like the strands of a spiderweb.

Still, the marks continued all the way to the far wall...to where a lone prum sat motionless.

It was Finn.

Not another soul was in sight, almost as though he'd been left behind.

"Ha-ha...ha-ha-ha-ha-ha...*gya-ha-ha-ha-ha-ha-ha-ha-ha-ha-ha-ha-ha-ha-ha!!*"

The prum captain's diminutive size made him look like an old doll whose owner had abandoned it, a sight that had Valletta positively roaring in laughter.

"Did your precious friends leave you, Finn? Did they decide they couldn't afford to protect you?! *Ha-ha-ha!!* What a riot!!"

Finn didn't respond, the shallow rise and fall of his chest the only indication that he was even alive. Valletta narrowed her eyes as she slowly went in for the kill.

—Suddenly, it came from her blind spot.

A certain young man leaped from the shadows. Concealing his breath, he waited for the precise moment when Valletta was in front of Finn before launching himself at her with the untapped ferocity of a beast.

"‼"

Gripping a shortsword in both hands, Raul went flying at Valletta.

"—Is that all?"

"Ngah?!"

But Valletta sidestepped his attack as easily as evading a child, grabbing ahold of his collar as he passed and slamming him to the ground.

The impact was enough to make his eyes roll back into his head as he tumbled faceup to the floor.

"Gngh…gah…"

"Forget my level, did ya, *High Novice*? As if your half-baked plan would work against a Level Five!" Valletta cackled, spitting on Raul as he lay spasming on the ground like a fish out of water. The sight was enough to make even the normally expressionless assassins sneer.

Valletta snorted. She remembered this little adventurer. "A real good-for-nothin' you've got workin' for ya, Finn. Almost makes me feel sorry for you, ha-ha-ha-ha-ha-ha!!"

The peal of laughter rang in their ears.

Across from her, Finn sluggishly raised his head—and smiled.

It was a tiny smile, the corners of his mouth moving only slightly, but it was a smile all the same.

"What are you laughing at…? Finn?"

It was the infuriating smile of a hero, the expression that had persisted so tenaciously in her memory.

As she began to seethe in barely contained rage, Finn's lips parted.

"…Good-for…nothing? My band is made up of…nothing but…heroes…"

Valletta let out another snort. "Heroes? Don't make me laugh! Or are you as blind as you are dumb—?" she started, only for her mockery to be cut short.

At the center of her gaze was Raul, still splayed out on the ground like a limp starfish. Tears had gathered in the corners of his eyes as he blubbered out a nearly inaudible soliloquy of self-reproach.

"No good...I'm no good...not even when they needed me most... Forgive me, Captain...for getting you involved in this...and sorry, Mom, but...but I'm not ready to die yet...!"

Sword lost, he instead tightened his grip around a small fist-size bag.

"Hey, High Novice! Just what do you think you're up to over—?"

Only she wasn't able to finish her thought.

"Lady Valletta! They have reinforcements!"

"!"

At the sudden shout from one of the assassins, she whirled around to see a catgirl rushing toward her from one of the other tunnels. And she wasn't the only one, either—there were three more from each of the remaining paths, and all of them were coming straight at her.

What the hell are they—?

She froze.

"_____"

From behind Aki, her sweat flying as she hurled herself down the tunnel, was the biggest swarm of monsters Valletta had ever seen.

While her attention had been focused on Finn, the other members of his group had been racing through the surrounding passages, luring as many monsters as they could. All four of them were leading their own massive parade.

Valletta and her entire crew went wide-eyed with shock—a development that did not escape Raul, and he leaped to his feet before launching the bag in his hand in Valletta's direction.

"What the—?! That *smell*...! Ugh!!"

It was the "magic powder" they'd picked up in Meren.

The powder that was actually a ground-up mixture of magic stones Njǫrðr had used to attract the violas in the sea. The crystal dust now covering their bodies would encourage the spider monsters to charge *straight at Valletta and her assassins.*

"_____"

Horrified realization appeared in Valletta's eyes as Aki upped her pace, her three companions attempted to hold back tears, and the throng of monsters stampeded toward them from every direction.

Raul's decisive plan...

...was none other than a pass parade of life-or-death proportions.

"Watch out, Raul!!"

In an instant, Aki leaped toward the assassins before bounding right over their heads.

And, just as planned, the monsters charging behind her set their sights on their new prey, dusted in magic-stone powder from head to toe—.

"Y-you've gotta be kidding meeeeeeeeeeeeeeeeeeeeeeeeeeeeeeeee!!!!!"

The hellish feast had begun.

As Valletta's scream ripped through the air, the horde of spiders lunged. It was like an avalanche as Aki's companions followed her lead and passed off their own parades, leading the teeming throng of monsters straight into the intersection.

"Captain!!" Raul screamed as he dove toward Finn, snatching him up into his arms as blood and other monster juices began raining down.

The enemies' monster-deceiving crystal did nothing anymore. Not in the face of the powder now coating their bodies. The horde of water spiders saw nothing but fresh meat as they besieged the assassins, fangs ripping and tearing and filling the tunnel with screams of agony. The assassins fought back desperately, whirling in every direction in an attempt to thwart their attacks as wave after wave of the beasts moved in for the kill.

It had been a gift from Loki.

A "just-in-case" sort of item for if they ran into trouble within the enemy stronghold, and a way for them to incite chaos between human and monster alike.

"Goddammiiiiiiiiiiit!!"

Not even a first-tier adventurer like Valletta could last long against the sheer mass of monsters attacking her now—a major miscalculation, considering she'd been ridiculing the same adventurers only a few moments prior.

Valletta and her forces had forgotten one important thing:

This was a Dungeon. And in the Dungeon, monsters made the rules.

There were no absolutes when it came to the labyrinth, and the vargs just kept on coming.

As if to further spur on the unforgiving pandemonium of the battle, Aki abruptly launched herself at Valletta.

"?!"

Valletta barely had time to react, still twisting desperately as her sword and claws bit into monster hide. And Aki took full advantage of her plight, lightsword flying as she raced toward the demoness with the "key."

"Don't you mess with meeeeeeeeeeeeeeee!!"

But Valletta was still a Level 5.

And using her Level-5 strength, she was able to fling the incoming monsters away, turning her attention to the incoming assailant.

"Ngh!!"

Aki stayed calm until the very end, even as Valletta's attacks bombarded her.

Following up every powerful strike with a swipe of her lightsword, she spun around with the grace of a cat. Then, after sidestepping the next counterattack, she aimed a blow straight at the vertebrae in Valletta's neck.

"Gngh?!"

Valletta's eyes popped open as she was sent crumbling to the ground.

Raul was right behind her.

"_____"

As the young man came at her with his dagger, the words of her mortal enemy rang through her head once more.

—"...Good-for...nothing? My men are...nothing but...heroes..."

The hunter had become the hunted—an outcome borne from

sheer desperation and an unstoppable resolve to outrun the touch of death. *Loki Familia*'s Level-4 "flunkies" had launched a combination attack reminiscent of Finn's and Riveria's handiwork.

Utilizing the opening Aki had created for him, Raul sent his dagger flying.

"Gngh!!"

"Nnnggaah?!"

Its blade carved a diagonal slash across her upper torso.

At the same time, the "key" slipped from her hand.

"Shi———!!"

Before she had a chance to snatch it back, it disappeared beneath a thundering landslide of spindly spider legs and claws. As she stumbled forward with a voiceless scream, Raul responded with a cry of his own, features twisting in urgency.

"*Retreeeeeeeaaaat! Everyone, RUN!!*"

With their number one target gone, *Loki Familia* had lost all reason to stay.

Darting in and out among the assassins and monsters, Raul sped away from the clamor, joining up with Aki and the rest of the group in a frantic sprint toward the tunnel Valletta had first appeared from.

"They're getting away! After them! *After theeeeeeeeeeeeem!!*" Valletta shrieked, but her assassins paid her no heed. They were far too busy defending themselves against the spider onslaught, and Raul's group slipped right past them before they could respond.

"*Fiiiiiiiiiiiiiiiiiiiiiiiiiiiiiiiiiiiiiiiiiiiiiiiiiiiiiiiiiiiiiiiiinnnnnnn nnn!!*"

The scream thundered down the tunnel behind them.

"Raul, are you okay?!"

"*Okay*'s a bit of a strong word, but I'm…gettin' by!"

As they made their escape, Aki fell in step beside Raul, who still had Finn in his arms. And it wasn't just Raul who was looking worse for the wear, either—Aki, Finn, all of them were covered in cuts and bruises, but that didn't lessen their speed. They'd made it. Finn was fine. Not that they had time to celebrate successfully outwitting their foes as they quickly continued down the tunnel.

Especially when Knossos wasn't about to let the adventurers escape.

Farther down the passage in front of them came the sound of a door opening, and suddenly, a massive swarm of violas launched themselves into the tunnel.

"?!"

Raul felt his breath catch. The timing was too perfect to be a coincidence.

Indeed, this was the work of none other than Barca, who had been spying on them from the watery film of the pedestal. Though neutralizing Finn and his crew had been entrusted to Valletta, after witnessing Raul's scheme, Barca had had no choice but to take matters into his own hands.

—Raul could practically feel the despair.

The wounded boy could almost hear their hearts breaking behind him.

From one menace to the next, the labyrinth wasn't done with them, its malice wringing from their hearts what hope they still had left.

Though the winds of favor currently propelled them forward, if they lost its graces now, they'd never be able to find them again.

"*Grrrrruuuuuuuuuuuaaaaaarrrrrrrrrrggggggggggghhhhhhhhhhhh!!*"

The earsplitting roar shook the walls as the massive beasts came charging.

"Take the captain!" Raul screamed in response, his eyes flashing.

"Raul?!"

But he'd already passed off the prum, launching himself forward toward the incoming stampede at an exhilarating speed. Snatching a short spear and dagger from one of his companions, he lunged, leaving Aki in shock behind him.

"*We push forward!!*"

It was a suicide attack.

The sight was one his companions were all too familiar with.

They'd seen it before—with Finn, with Aiz, with all the other first-tier elites.

"Ruuuuaaaaaaaaaaaaggghhh!!"

Only this time it was a Level-4 second-tier in their place.

Spear sailing and sword gleaming, Raul flew, cutting through the mass of tentacles and splitting heads left and right.

But there were simply too many of them, and no sooner had he finished his first attack than the monsters sent their tentacles toward him en masse. Blood ran rivers down his forehead; his fingers cracked; ugly bright-red rivulets spilled from his nostrils.

He'd reached his limit.

But who had expected otherwise?

He wasn't a first-tier adventurer, after all. He wasn't like Finn and the others.

"————Nnnggh!!"

But that didn't stop him.

For every time he was struck, he retaliated viciously and shattered magic stones, building piles of ash around him as he forced a way open for the rest of his party.

"Stop, Raul!!" Aki screamed from behind him.

But he didn't look back, no matter how many times she cried out, and swung his weapons again and again and again.

"You're going to kill yourself…!!"

"This is what the captain would do!"

"You're not the captain!!" she screamed, so loud her voice cracked.

"You don't think I know that?!" Raul's response was immediate and powerful, stunning her into silence. "I'll…never be like him! I'll never be like all those people we look up to!"

Raul knew his place all too well.

He was indecisive. A pitiful excuse for a human being. No one in the familia, not even his juniors, considered him remotely noteworthy. He could run himself ragged, but he'd never compare to Finn, Aiz, and the other first-tiers.

—Doesn't matter how hard I try. I'll never be like them. I know that.

His vision was starting to warp. It took him a moment to realize there were tears in his eyes. Tears of anguish. His confidence was failing him, stolen by the cruel vision of those chosen few ahead of him.

He was useless. Completely, utterly useless.

"But…" He wiped the blood and snot from his nose with his arm as he drew it back for a jab with his spear. "…I'll be even more useless if…if I stop chasing them now!" he cried out, tears threatening to spill from his eyes as he squeezed them shut.

Just as Lefiya had a dream of her own to chase…

…he, too, struggled to keep up with his own target.

"You idiot…!" Aki called, salt stinging her eyes as she took out the enemies to her left and right in an attempt to shield Raul from the onslaught of tentacles.

"*Ruuuuuaaaaaarrrggghhh!!*"

Raul sent his spear spiraling into the odious jaw of the final viola.

With a crisp *snap*, the haft broke in two, but not before the spearhead shattered the magic stone deep inside the creature's flesh. Just before its teeth came down around him, the monster disintegrated into a pile of ash.

"Come on! Let's get movin'! We can't stop now!!" Raul bellowed, his body liable to give out at any moment.

"*Y-yeeahhhhh!!*" His companions raised a triumphant roar, hot on his heels as he abandoned his broken spear and unsheathed a longsword.

"…Kids these…days…" Finn rasped from the base of his throat.

"Captain?" The girl carrying him turned around. The prum captain was laughing, faintly but surely, from behind the rest of the group.

"You're already a…fine adventurer…Raul."

Graceless and unseemly though their struggle was, the adventurers would refuse to succumb.

"Miss Tiona!"

The synchronous deluge of poison vermis attacks shot through the air.

Elfie's eyes squeezed shut in anticipation of her gruesome end.

"...?"

Only the blow never came.

Instead, she heard a raging gale, surging up and in and all throughout the tunnel.

Ever so slowly, she cracked her eyes open before gazing in wonder at what she saw.

"Not...todaaaaaaay!!"

Tiona was wielding her Urga in one hand, spinning it like the blade of a windmill.

The cyclone it created was so powerful, so fast, it acted as a force field that sent the incoming wave of vermis toxin flying in every direction. Still, not a single drop hit the adventurers behind her.

"Cast something, guys!!" she screamed.

"!"

The magic users were stunned for a moment, then nodded in zealous affirmation.

In less than an instant, their chant began. It was so loud, it drowned out the cacophonous competition between toxin and sword mill. While the girls readied their staves, even the boy, injured as he was from previous exposure to the venom, raised his arm and gasped out his spell.

The moment the first drop of sweat fell from Tiona, still caught in her test of endurance with the multitude of maggots, their magic was ready.

"Miss Tiona!!"

"Let 'er rip!! One big blast!!!"

In coordinated precision they'd practiced time and time again during their expeditions, Tiona leaped out of the way the moment the mages on the back line let loose their magic blast. The poison vermis, seeing the line of defense gone, rushed forward, only to find themselves face-to-face with the perfectly timed inferno headed straight in their direction. It rushed through them, frying them on the spot.

"Gwww——————————uaaaaaaghhh!!"

Flames filled the tunnel as the three unique blazes completely swallowed the maggots' bodies. They atomized everything, forming a roaring sea of fire that left nothing but magic-stone cores in its wake.

"M-Miss Tiona, your—your hands!"

Having escaped the crisis temporarily, the three magic users looked now to Tiona's sword hand, eyes widening in horror.

Though the blade of her Urga had protected them from the toxins, her hand around its hilt hadn't been so lucky, taking the full brunt of the vermis venom. Her normally copper-colored skin had turned an intense shade of black.

"No biggie! You shoulda seen the stuff I got hit with in Meren—and I still kept fightin'!" Tiona laughed, shrugging off their tearful gazes with a reference to her duel against Bache, the Poison Queen. Despite the sweat pouring off her, she still wore her usual smile on her face.

"...Sorry, though. Kinda hard to...save everyone all by myself."

The sweat refused to stop.

Smile faltering, she looked out over her three teammates.

She didn't have Tione with her. Didn't have Finn or Gareth. Not even Aiz or Lefiya. Hell, she would have even taken Bete at this point. It was only her. And she was quickly realizing that not even a first-tier adventurer like her could free them from their current predicament all alone.

Her own stupidity, her inability to come up with a solution, was beginning to grate on her.

But without even trying to put on a brave face, she entreated, "So... if you could maybe...do the savin' for me...?" Her grin returned, sweat-drenched though it was.

The sight of her in such pain was enough to make Elfie and the others stop short before replying in unison:

""""*Roger!!*""""

"All right, then! Let's do this! We put our heads together and we'll make it through somehow!"

Even as their arms and legs trembled, the group felt smiles return to their faces.

Morale back with a vengeance, Tiona took off, leading them down the tunnel—and toward a lingering hope.

The assassin's mighty mace came flying at her.

At the sickening squelch of flesh, Cruz and the other supporters turned white in horror.

"————*Guagh!!*"

But it wasn't Tione who'd been shattered—it was the giant face of the assassin.

The Amazon's copper fist had connected with the bridge of his nose, splitting it in two and rendering it a squishy mess. Watching the action play out, her companions nearly fainted right there on the spot.

"B-but why…?" the giant figure moaned, snot and tears dribbling down over his shattered front teeth before he fell head over heels to the ground below. His mace, just like his face, had been smashed into thousands of tiny pieces.

The punishing fist of an Amazon never missed its mark.

"Because you've done nothing but…whine and moan…!" Tione flexed her fist, chunks of skin missing from her knuckles. Around her, no one moved, and a heavy silence settled over the passageway.

She'd just smashed through the man's mace at point-blank range. Gaze directed downward, she suddenly raised her head—murderous flames searing her eyes.

"And I'm sick of it!!"

In instant later, the massacre commenced.

Her fists flying, her feet slicing through the air like blades, she tore into the assassins; sprays of blood gushed from their mouths with each bone-crunching strike. She dealt with them exactly as she'd dealt with their giant leader, leaving them down for the count in one hit with no chance of waking up anytime soon.

As the string of desperate screams echoed up around them, the other assassins flew into a panic, unsure what to do.

"What's going on? Is the anti-Status Magic no longer working?!"

"B-but there's no wa—Aaaarrrrrrrrrrrrggggggggggghhhhhhhhhh!!"

But they weren't even given the time to finish their thoughts as Tione picked them off one by one. She didn't stop, and the multiple curses and anti-Status Magic seemingly did nothing against her onslaught.

It was a rampage of virtually unparalleled proportions.

"Oh, right…Her skill: Berserk," Cruz said as the memory of Tione's barbaric ability dawned on him.

It was an ability that drew from her building rage to greatly augment her physical strength. And given the underhanded way the assassins had pummeled her with debuff after debuff, it only made sense her anger levels would be practically off the charts. In fact, with each new curse or anti-Status Magic spell cast, her strength actually seemed to *grow*, completely reversing their status-lowering effects.

"I'm gonna tear you apart!!"

Tione's current speed might not have even been comparable to what she was truly capable of, but it was strong enough to take care of the throng of assassins. Closing in on them with uniform pressure, she unleashed fist and foot alike in a cyclone of blows.

Crunch! Snap! Thud! The nauseating sounds were enough to make anyone want to plug their ears. Even Cruz and the others found themselves instinctively curling their toes in horror at the scene of gut-wrenching violence and ceaseless screams.

"Hey! Where's that key, huh? Give it to me or I'll crush every bone in your damn body!!" She yanked up one of the half-dead assassins by his collar. Battered corpses lay in heaps at her feet like mountains towering over rivers of blood.

"I—I don't have it…! I'm not the one who shut the door—!"

"Useless!!"

She didn't even let him finish, slamming him down onto the floor and eliciting a garbled yelp of pain.

The sight of her standing there, shoulders heaving and fists drenched in blood, made Cruz and the others slowly back away.

"Bunch of pigs…All right, kids, any one of you so much as thinks of getting themselves killed and I'll rearrange your face!! Got it?!"

""Y-yes, ma'am!!"" they shouted back, unable to so much as move at the murderous gaze directed their way.

And so, like her sister, Tione raised the morale of her companions in her own way, and they dashed off to begin the journey home.

"...M-Mister Gareth!" Narfi's voice called out hoarsely.

Though the young girl's body had been slightly burned, she'd made it out of the incoming wave of flames alive. The others, too, had escaped with nothing more than light injuries. Splayed out on the ground, they looked up to see the heroic bare back of a dwarven warrior.

It was Gareth, giant shield at the ready, *bearing the full brunt of the inferno.*

"Quite a blaze...Gives a wall of a man like me a...run for his money...!" It was clearly a bluff, as smoke billowed up from his body while his battle clothes and armor charred beneath the flames. Still, despite everything, the dauntless grin never left his face.

After grabbing a shield from one of the supporters, he'd made his body into an impenetrable bulwark, shoving Narfi and the others to his rear in order to shelter them from the massive surge of fire.

"A-are you okay?! How are you even still standing right now?!"

"Some prum once told me this great lug of a body was the only thing I had goin' for me, y'know!"

"That didn't answer my question!!"

The ease with which he spoke gave no indication as to how long he'd continue to be able to endure the flames. And as they watched him, their eyes widened further still, and their mouths hung open.

Just what kind of adventurer would be able to withstand a direct hit from those flames? He didn't need tricks or schemes; his body was simply that strong, too strong, a state-of-the-art shield. And with it he had saved them from the vicious trap of fire.

This was going far beyond the line of duty, a fact that left Narfi and the rest of the group in a state of reverence.

"...? The door's opening...?!"

"Mister Gareth! Another trap!"

Almost as if it, too, were cowed by the dwarf's braggadocio, the door behind them rumbled open.

There was an explosion, followed by a second wall of flames. The new set of inferno stones ignited with a powerful blast, filling the second tunnel with blinding light and sending an onrush of searing-hot air down the passage toward them.

"Ah, so impatient. I'm afraid I'll have to decline. One course is enough for me. Narfi! Take the shield, lass!"

"Huh? I—Understood, sir!"

Watching Narfi and the others move into position, Gareth shifted his shoulders, standing directly in front of the labyrinth wall. A moment later, the wall burst, stone and pebble scattering to reveal the adamantite beneath. And it was in that moment that he struck—using every bit of strength he had left in his body—to smash through the glimmering metal.

"?!"

A crack worked its way up through the wall. In a single strike of the dwarf's fist, the adamantite had parted—an act that made Narfi's and the others' eyes go wide, but which paled in comparison to his next move. Both hands curling into balled fists, he launched himself at the wall, striking it a thousand times over in a mad rush of blows.

"Guuuuuuuuuuuuuuuuuuuurrrrrrrrrrrooooooooooooooooooooooo ooooooaaaaaaaaaaaaaaaaaaaaaaaaaaaaaaaaaaaaaaaa*aaaaaaaaaaAAAAA AAAAAAAAARRRRRRRRRRRRRRRRRRRRRRGGGGGGHHHHHH*!!"

It was a feat of strength that took the dwarf back to his roots. Each thunderous punch of his fist released an earsplitting crack, scarcely discernible from magic, as he wore away more and more of the adamantite wall. The supposedly indestructible surface caved deeper and deeper, groaning and shivering beneath the dwarf's rapid barrage. He may as well have been mining ore the way he went to work, chipping away piece after piece of the ironlike bulwark until—finally—it gave way with a shudder.

A window into the tunnel next to theirs opened up before him.

"Up and at 'em! Get off those bums and into that hole!"

And so they did, slipping into the safety of the connecting tunnel with barely more than a second to spare before the wall of flame engulfed the passageway behind them.

It was a tight fit, and by the time they emerged from the other side, they seemed unsure if they were witnessing reality and simply stood for a moment in dazed silence.

"M-Mister Gareth, your hands..." Narfi sobbed.

"Oh, this? A flesh wound is all! Nothin' a quick potion won't fix right up."

"Y-yes, but..."

Gareth glanced at his fists himself, both of them dyed red with blood around the undeniable white of exposed bone peeking through the skin. Then, tossing aside his melted shield, he urged the group forward as though nothing was wrong. "Let's get goin' then, ye greenhorns! No point waitin' around for the next trap to come!"

"...I'm starting to think that so long as Mister Gareth's here, we'll make it out alive," one of Narfi's companions muttered next to her.

"I-I can't disagree there, but—we can't just let him do everything! C'mon, we've gotta figure out something we can do, too! Do we wanna be first-tiers someday or not?!" she shot back.

"Your voice is cracking, Narfi..."

Running out in front of them, Gareth furrowed his brows.

I mighta pulled us outta this scrape by the skin o' my teeth, but aught as like I couldn't pull it off again soon...We need to find a way out, or we're done for. He raced down the halls of the amaranthine labyrinth, fumbling with the bag tied around his waist. He snatched up one of the few high potions he had left and doused his fists in the healing liquid.

Reconvene with Finn an' the others...Find the exit...Gods almighty, we've not suffered such dire straits in years!

"What'sa matter, Vanargand? Don't tell me you're just gonna let 'em all die?"

Dix called out with a peal of laughter. Within the tunnel itself, friend and foe alike continued to rage at one another like crazed beasts.

"Shit..." Bete cursed beneath his breath as he watched the action unfold from within his small offshoot from the main passage. If he had any hope of attacking Dix, he'd need to get across that war zone first. But even if he did make it through unscathed, the same couldn't be said for his companions, who would carry on their maddened frenzy until they were devoid of strength.

Even watching their indiscriminate flailing now, he could see their wounds accumulating. As a friend's sword tip met the flesh of a girl's arm, she screamed like a wild animal, but still they continued, never once laying down their arms.

"Guys?!" Rakuta fretted nervously next to him, the only other one to escape the effects of Dix's Phobetor Daedalus curse.

They didn't have much time left. Spitting out one last swear, Bete turned his gaze toward the hooded man with a vindictive glare.

Whew, you really wanna kill me, don'tcha? The curse'll be kaput if you just take down its caster—you must have figured it out by now? Dix thought, eyes narrowing beneath goggles and hood. He could practically feel the animus radiating from the tunnel where Bete currently hid, even from the thirty-or-so-meder distance between them.

The wolf was guarding himself against his curse—of that he was certain.

Dix was only a Level 5. If he were to go up against Bete in traditional hand-to-hand combat, Bete had the clear advantage.

But none of that mattered in the face of Dix's curse; not even the strongest, highest-ranked Level 6 in all of Orario could outlast a direct hit from his curse.

If he waits things out and watches his friends hack one another to pieces, then I can simply close one of these doors and make my escape. And if he decides to try and help 'em, well, I'll just curse him! Even against a Level 6 like him, it should be an easy kill.

Dix couldn't use his Phobetor Daedalus a second time without lifting his current instance of the curse first, but even with that, the distance between him and Bete now would give him plenty of time to cast it again without fear of the werewolf reaching him first.

No matter what, Dix was about to have Vanargand's head mounted on his wall.

The goggled man snorted with laughter at his own ingenuity.

"Not gonna come out and play? Pssshht, what a piss-poor excuse for a Level Six!"

As Dix continued to taunt him from across the hall, Bete's ashen fur bristled. Then, in the instant it took the emotion to leave his face, he suddenly appeared at the center of the melee.

"Gotcha." Dix sneered as he pointed directly at the wolf.

"Mister Bete!!" Rakuta screamed as she watched her peers set their sights on Bete.

"Gwwwuuuaaaaaaarrrrrrrrrggggghh!!"

They pounced, monster and adventurer alike, on their new prey.

And as for Bete...

"Aww, shut the hell up already!!" he spit in annoyance before latching his claws onto the face of an incoming animal girl—*and slamming her into the ground.*

"_____"

Neither Dix nor Rakuta moved.

The force was so great, it cracked the floor below, and the girl's arms and legs instantly went limp.

He didn't stop there. He attacked everything, butchering incoming monsters left and right, flinging his fellow *Loki Familia* members into the walls and floor.

——*What the hell is wrong with this guy?!*

The looks of shocked horror that crossed Dix's and Rakuta's faces were identical as they watched him fell friend and foe alike.

"Sleep it off, you worthless pieces of shit!"

He'd discovered the one tactic that worked against Dix's Phobetor Daedalus—*putting down its victims.* By completely eliminating his rampaging peers from the picture, eliminating any reserves he had about harming them, he was able to render the curse ineffective.

There was no need to worry about breaking the curse if there was no one left to curse.

It was certainly a simple, immediate solution to the problem at hand.

The question, however, lay in one's ability to actually carry it out.

——*This guy really is an asshole.*

Even Dix found himself shaken at the werewolf's complete disregard for his own companions, and in the few seconds it took him to collect his thoughts, Bete had already taken care of every monster and every adventurer in the tunnel—and was now *closing in on him.*

"Ngh?!"

Bete came at a speed Dix could never have imagined.

But he still had time.

The wolf was already in Dix's sights, and though his chest clenched with fear, the smile returned to his goggled face as he released the curse.

"*Get lost in an endless nightma——!*"

But then.

His chant was cut off.

And his expression was frozen in place.

——*Hey now.*

In fact, time seemed to have stopped completely.

Because in that single instant, the distance between the wolf and him seemed to have vanished. Now he was staring him down at point-blank range as a single realization blossomed in his mind. If he were to use his Phobetor Daedalus curse on Bete now, who would be the berserk wolf's first target?

No, really. *Who would be right in front of him?*

The fresh meat dangling in front of the crazed, rampaging, feral wolf would be none other than—

——*?!*

Dix himself.

It couldn't be anyone *but* Dix.

There was no one else. No monsters, no humans. It would be a one-on-one duel to the death. Bete's momentum would propel his fangs straight into the body immediately ahead to devour him.

At this distance, his curse was *absolutely useless.*

———*Damn.*

Bete had planned everything. He'd taken into account both Dix's speed and the strength and nature of the Phobetor Daedalus curse. He'd eliminated his target's every option in one full-powered attack of indescribable speed.

It was the zeal of a man willing to sign his own death warrant—no, a man who'd bet everything for the sake of victory.

His amber eyes were on fire with a scarcely contained vengeance. Dix's smile crumbled.

An instant later, the wolf's metal boots connected with his chest.

For just a moment, he was overcome with horror. Then Bete bared his teeth.

"You said you wanted to play, didn'tcha?"

His fist came at him so fast he couldn't even see it.

"Gaahh?!"

Dix doubled over in an almost graceful curve.

Then, the wolf howled, releasing all the pent-up fury that had been building inside him.

"Ruuuuuuuuuuuusssaaaaaaaaaaarrrrrrrrrrrrrggggggggghhhhhhhh!!"

"————————————————?!"

His feet, his fists, his elbows, everything assailed him at once.

Dix didn't even have a chance to defend himself, much less cast one of his short spells. Blood sprayed from his mouth as the bones in his arms snapped like twigs, and his field of vision flicked this way and that over and over.

The wolf's relentless assault was carving away his life.

And as Bete's fangs sunk into his windpipe, a single emotion raced through his mind.

Fear.

For the first time in his life, the cruel, contemptuous hunter feared death.

———*Shit, shit, shit—!!*

Veins in his eyes popping, he felt his instincts scream in urgency. Using what little strength he had left, not even caring what he looked like at this point, he pushed himself back and away.

"!"

It was his first and final act of resistance, taking advantage of Bete's attacks to launch himself away and successfully free himself from the Level 6.

Naturally, Bete followed.

With the wolf hot on his heels, Dix raised his face from the floor, red eye glinting from beneath his goggles.

"Get back here, you goddamn—!!"

That instant, the orichalcum door fell.

"!!"

Bete had reached out to stop him, but his hand was in the wrong place at the wrong time.

Like a guillotine, the thick wall slammed it into the ground below.

"Ha...ha-ha...ha-ha-ha-ha-ha-ha-ha-ha-ha-ha-ha-ha-ha!!" Dix cackled from the other side of the door. "Too bad, Vanargand! You almost had me, too!"

While the rivers of sweat running down his temples were evidence enough of his emotions, he was relieved both inside and out now that he was safe. Not only that, his enemy's arm had been crushed beneath the door. No doubt, even at this very moment, Bete was howling and writhing in pain on the other side. Either that, or he'd torn the arm off altogether.

"Ahh, shit, I'm not in much better shape myself...! Damn, that smarts! What a shit show...!!"

He used his crimson spear as a crutch—he hadn't even had time to use the damn thing to protect himself earlier—to push himself to his feet, though his battered, bruised body groaned at him from beneath his robed disguise.

"But at least I've got this on my side...!" His tune changed as he glanced at the orichalcum door in question, his lips turning up.

Until the door gave a sudden rumble.

He looked down to see a very visible *space* between the door and the ground.

"_____"

Grrrrrrnnnnnnnnn... The noise continued as slowly, little by little, the door began to rise.

Dix found himself frozen in place.

Hey, moron, you even know how heavy that door is—?

But already, the world on the other side was peeping through—a view of two powerful legs in metallic boots and a wolf's tail swishing back and forth.

In what was probably the most surprising of the building developments, the wolf was using a single arm, crushed gauntlet and all, to lift the barricade from its resting place.

Before Dix knew it, the door was up to his chest...and he was staring into the bloodshot amber eyes of an enraged werewolf.

"Guh?!"

At this point, there was no other option—he ran.

Whirling around on his heels, he took off down the tunnel, pushing his mangled body as fast as it would go.

"Goddamn Barca...! You really expect me to go toe-to-toe with this guy again?!" he cursed as he limped into the maze.

"Shit, he got away..." Bete's brows furrowed in annoyance as he watched Dix disappear down the passage. "Hey! We'll go this way! And bring those guys with you—hurry!"

"You've gotta be kidding me!"

As Bete gave his orders, still supporting the weight of the door, Rakuta moaned and dragged the limp bodies of her companions behind her.

There was a roar as the wind around her was ripped to pieces.

As the shreds of her air currents scattered, screaming into the ether, the golden locks of her blood-smeared hair danced.

The slender swordswoman's body sailed through the air.

"_____?!"

She crashed into the floor with tremendous force and went tumbling across the room, until finally, she came to a stop among the tangled mesh of pipes lining the ground.

Trembling, using her sword for balance, she tried to struggle to her feet, but her knees lacked the strength. Her armor no longer did her any good now that pieces of it were missing. Between the tatters of her battle clothes, the wounds on her supple flesh were clearly exposed, and blood from her head formed a river across the eyelid of one of her beautiful golden eyes, now squeezed shut.

She was barely hanging on.

"You're tenacious. I'll give you that..." Levis commented as she made her way over.

She was not without injury herself. Similar to Aiz, her battle clothes had turned to rags, and several of the wounds inflicted by Aiz's wind sword were frighteningly deep.

However, she had one thing going for her that Aiz didn't—a cloud of steam surrounding her body, floating particles of magic that steadily healed the gashes littering her skin.

It was her self-recovery skill, an especially aggravating healing ability possessed by creatures, and seeing her work come to nothing at the hand of those mist-like particles made Aiz grimace in frustration.

Just how many magic stones had this monstrosity devoured?

"You're strong, too, to keep fighting even after the blow you suffered."

Around them, the room was in a state of disarray, evidence of the savage duel that had taken place. Pipes had been tossed about, their surfaces cracked and leaking fluid out onto the floor. The tanks, too, scarcely resembled tanks any longer, their glass fractured and strewn about the perimeter.

Chest heaving, Aiz tried to ready her sword for another onslaught, only for Levis to rebuff her efforts. Stepping forward, the red-haired woman grabbed her by the face and slammed her into the wall.

"Unngaaagh!!"

Cracks spread out from the point of impact as one of the large tanks shattered with a high-pitched screech.

The wind was knocked from her lungs as numbing spasms ran through her arms and legs like jolts of electricity. Levis didn't stop there, wildly swinging her left arm to sling Aiz back to the floor as though she was nothing.

"Nnnguh...?!"

"But I'm getting tired of this pointless back-and-forth. Aren't you?"

Levis's voice was like ice against her ear as she lay there, moaning into the ground.

A pointless back-and-forth. It certainly was, at this point.

First in Rivira, then in the pantry, and now, finally, here in Knossos.

A humiliating defeat followed by relentless pursuit. Being slammed to the ground but always rising tall, back for more...Yes, this fight of theirs had been going on for some time now.

And once again, today, Aiz found herself on the brink of death.

"Let's end this."

The footsteps that would spell her destruction grew near.

All of a sudden, Aiz's consciousness sparked back to life.

...Have to...stand...My sword...I have to...I can't...

Her thoughts were a muddled mess. Her body burned with blood and pain. But somewhere, within that haze of her mind, she found that last thread of her will to fight, furrowing her forehead as she forced it out.

She could see the little girl inside her hugging herself as she wept, but she turned away, reaching instead for the sword standing in the darkness—to the Sword Princess, Aiz Wallenstein. She shouted at her arms and legs, though they threatened to give out completely, and pulled her Desperate toward her from where it lay on the ground.

"...That's enough, Aria. There's no use struggling."

Levis's emotionless voice echoed around her again.

"You cannot win as you are now. And no one is coming for you. This ridiculous labyrinth has seen to that. It is the monster that will devour you, as it's already done to your companions, no doubt."

Sccrrrrr. Aiz's fingers clawed at the floor.

"There's no one to save you now."

—*I know that.*

Yes, Aiz knew that all too well.

Help wasn't coming for her. No hands to pull her to her feet. No sword to stave off the coming death.

No hero to save her.

The hero she had longed for, ever since her father protected her mother, had never come.

She was all alone.

Despair had been her everything. She had wailed and cried and screamed until she could cry no more. Until her heart was frozen and she could no longer remember how to smile.

It had been then that Aiz had taken up the sword.

She wouldn't wait to be saved. She would carve her own path, the only one left in front of her.

She would hunger after power, and even now she pursued it with reckless abandon.

So that she could fulfill her one true desire, her deepest wish, her heart's yearning.

It was all that was left in the hollow shell she'd become.

She'd had no one. No knight in shining armor.

Until—.

"—But now..."

Arms trembling, she peeled her battered body away from the floor.

As blood dripped down, her slender legs pushed her to her feet.

And then her closed eye popped wide with a snap.

"...I'm not alone...anymore."

She had friends who cared about her. Adorable rookies who

looked up to her. Dependable allies who fought beside her. Caring adults who watched over her like their own children.

A compassionate familia, merry and cheerful, that taught her how to smile again.

And she had an irreplaceable bond. A home that she never, ever wanted to lose again.

"So...I won't give up!"

As Levis's brows arched in surprise, Aiz reached her feet with her sword at the ready. With glimmering golden eyes, she stared down her avenger, who had come back stronger and more powerful than ever.

*You've won...and I'm okay with that...*she conceded, painful as it was for her to admit.

She would swear an oath to her sword in pursuit of an even greater power.

But if there's one thing I won't let you take from me...it's them.

They were the one thing she refused to give up.

Though the Sword Princess, who'd never sought anything save strength, was willing to admit defeat, Aiz herself was not willing to lose the lives of the ones she held dear.

Readying her sword as a knight once more, she closed her eyes.

Levis was an enhanced species; what's more, she commanded power well over that of a Level 7. Even with her wind, Aiz couldn't hope to contend with her. Outwitting her at this point would be close to impossible. Physically, her wounds were already deep. Her body would be unable to take another skirmish.

But she still had one thing—her Mind.

"——This is it."

She would ignite her very essence, the flames of what little life she had left.

Her enemy was Levis.

No. Aiz had already lost to her.

She was now facing someone else, someone bigger—the labyrinth itself.

"Awaken, Tempest!"

Her eyes snapped open.

"Awaken, Tempest!!"

She shouted again, ignoring her battered body as she cloaked herself once more in the howl of the wind torn from her.

"RAGE, TEMPEST!!"

She shouted a third time.

And with it came a gale, unleashing a fury that mirrored the sleeping power awakening inside her.

"What the—?"

It was more furious than any Airiel Aiz had summoned before.

As it filled the room, it slashed the pipes to shreds before rushing into the tunnels beyond. And it didn't stop there, billowing out relentlessly from her as if it were rolling off a hill.

"The wind of the great spirit..." Levis's eyes narrowed.

Was the swordswoman using it to protect herself? To keep Levis at bay? Then it would do her no good to approach recklessly now. Surely, with the way Aiz was spending magic power like water, she would destroy herself soon enough; however, the ferocious gale had yet to show any signs of waning.

On and on, it raged, fueled by the fires of Aiz's very soul.

"If you keep this up...!"

—She might awaken the spirit embryos lurking deep within the halls of the maze. Realizing this, Levis moved toward Aiz, her expression twisting in irritation. Like a blade, she cut through the incoming winds, sword aimed straight at the Sword Princess.

But Aiz met her head-on, raising Desperate to accept the incoming strike. Her storm didn't so much as sputter at the movement as she first blocked, then fled from the attack like a tornado on the move.

"You!...Stop squirming!"

"Gngh!"

Again and again, Aiz's piercing wind hindered Levis's strikes. The creature woman simply couldn't take her down, even with the heavy injuries she'd inflicted. With the gale dampening her speed and power, Levis's every attack was countered by the Sword Princess's own techniques. There were no blind spots, either; the raging squall swelled in every direction, to the point where Levis had to devote her concentration merely to keep from blowing away.

This wasn't armor anymore. This was a fortress. And Levis was clearly becoming increasingly irritated as she continued her attack.

Not...yet...!

Aiz would hold out.

Her windstorm seethed, and she threw everything she had into staving off Levis's fury.

Aiz would wait.

Until her cyclone had proved victorious against that labyrinth of chaos.

Hold out. Hold out. Hold out.

Wait. Wait. Wait.

She was betting everything, her own life, on this foolhardy defensive plan that was only postponing her inevitable death, or so it seemed.

All the while, her wind *raised its great war cry.*

"Just go down——*quietly*!!"

"Nngugh?!"

Levis's blade finally met its mark.

The downward slash cleaved through Aiz's armor of wind, and though Aiz just barely managed to bring her Desperate up in time to block, the force was simply too much, knocking the sword from her hands.

One of Aiz's knees thumped to the ground, signaling her limit. And with it, her wind grew silent.

"Any further resistance will only draw this out far longer than it needs to...Now, since I'm going to strip you of your consciousness anyway, let's cut off your limbs to make sure you can't get up to anything else."

Aiz squinted at the figure towering over her.

A moment before the other woman's sword descended.

Tap.

The very discernible sound of a footstep reverberated through the room.

"…Who's there?" Levis cried out as she whirled around, only to stop in her tracks.

Meanwhile, as Aiz was fighting for her life for the last time in the hall of tanks…

"Miss Tiona, Arcus won't last much longer…!"

"…Well, crap."

Tiona and the rest of her party were run ragged with exhaustion, having faced a multitude of monsters and plenty of traps, to boot.

And now? They'd run out of options.

Nothing but endlessly winding halls, pointlessly claustrophobic stone, and mocking shadow surrounded them. They were sapped of strength, worn to the bone from damage, and worst of all, clueless as to where they should go—and their weary hearts were slowly crumbling to pieces.

At least in the Dungeon they'd had a map.

They'd known what to expect as far as monsters and traps went, and where they could go if they needed to rest.

They had none of that in this man-made labyrinth of death. To say nothing of the malicious doors that continuously opened and closed on them, sealing their every means of escape.

They were isolated, cut off from anyone who might help them. Despair weighed heavily on their shoulders, an invisible enemy, and their faces reflected the belief that they were forever trapped in the endless winding halls of their labyrinthine prison.

Not even Tiona's smile could rescue the group's dwindling morale now.

Sweat poured from her face and her male companion's, both suffering from the poison vermis venom.

When suddenly.

"Is that…wind?" Elfie murmured beneath Arcus's weight as the tiniest of breezes tickled her skin. Next to her, Tiona came to a stop.

Yes, the air was stirring. It felt different from the stagnant maze.

It tapped at her Urga, running up its smooth blade before curling against her cheek.

Something was calling them.

A...breeze?

It whispered against her ear with gentle footsteps, causing her eyes to widen with a start.

When, only a moment later——*PHWOOOOOOOOW!!*

Wind began roaring through the tunnel, unleashing waves of raw power.

"What the—?!"

"_____?!"

The surge was so powerful, it sent Elfie and the rest of the group stumbling backward, bending over in an attempt to stay on their feet.

It was a hurricane, lashing at their cheeks, pulling at their weapons, and violently tousling their hair.

It was a breath, unrelenting yet full of warmth, to blow away the darkness of the labyrinth.

"What the...hell...is this?!"

"Another trap?!"

"——No," Tiona said simply, lifting her face as the rest of her group balked at the unimaginably powerful winds. Because with the wind came a voice, a serene, gentle voice that brought visions to her mind's eye.

Amber wheat, gently drifting clouds, and a spirit, its lips moving in song——a golden-haired maiden racing down a windy hilltop.

The wind was calling them.

"It's Aiz!" she cried out as the smile returned to her fatigued face.

And then the instinct-driven Amazonian girl was sprinting down the passage.

"Aiz is calling us!"

"Miss Tione, this wind! What is it...?!"

Meanwhile, in another section of the maze, Tione, Cruz, and the rest of her group had also encountered the storm.

"Ah——"

As her long hair whipped about her face, light spread across Tione's features.

The raging, ceaseless wind had summoned a memory in her mind, too.

"This is…Aiz! This is Aiz's wind!!"

——*Caves in the mountains were rife with drafts, so it was easy to use 'em as guideposts.*

——*Basically, ye either follow the wind or ye run counter to it. That's how to avoid winding up at a dead end.*

Yes, that was what they'd been talking about when they'd first stepped foot into this labyrinth. It was exactly as Gareth had told them. They could use drafts as guideposts.

Of course, there wouldn't be any *natural* drafts running through the man-made dungeon directly below the city's surface. Instead, the wind racing past them now was being created by Aiz's Airiel.

"She's leading us! She's telling us where we are…and where we can join up with the others!"

Aiz's powerful gusts left no trace of the maze untouched, pulsing through its every nook and cranny like blood pumping through veins. It was a positively ludicrous feat, one that Tione herself could barely believe—and yet, this was Aiz. Aiz *would* be able to do something like this, and that thought alone brought a brilliant smile to her face.

Even separated as they were by crossroad after crossroad, Aiz had been able to create one single road to lead them together. *This way,* the wind seemed to cry. It would lead them straight to Aiz as a rallying call for all of *Loki Familia* currently trapped within that massive labyrinth.

Tione would answer that call, racing off down the tunnel with the others hot on her heels.

"Let's go!"

"Right behind you!!"

"That reckless girl! She's up to this tomfoolery again, I see!"

Gareth fumed, facing the wind filling up the grand hall head-on.

"You mean...Aiz? This is Aiz's wind...? But that's...that's impossible!" Narfi yelped in disbelief.

It was true. To think that a single adventurer would be able to reach the entirety of this massive dungeon was simply preposterous.

But that was exactly what was happening, and the ridiculous power behind Aiz's Airiel and the girl's own swordlike spirit was enough to put her on par with a floor boss.

However, Gareth realized something—that Aiz was burning her very life force to create this guiding path of wind. She had to be, or she'd never be able to produce a gale like this. Which could mean only one thing: that she'd gone and gotten herself in grave danger again.

"That aside, now's no time for loiterin'!" Gareth cried out to the rest of the group, wind whistling past the cracks in his heavy armor. "Up and at 'em, greenhorns! We lose that wind and we'll have no chance!"

"What the hell is all this wind?!"

The same gust was blowing past Valletta and the rest of her enemy troops, as well. She snapped an arm up to cover her face with a groan as the violent gale whipped against her.

"Raul!"

"You read my mind!"

Not far away, Aki and Raul, still wandering about the maze, grabbed Finn and ran in the direction of the howling cyclone, too.

"Mister Bete, not so...fast...!"

"Grr!"

"M-Mister Bete?!"

Bete, too, made an abrupt about-face at the sudden appearance of Aiz's storm. Behind him, Rakuta attempted desperately to match his breakneck pace with the rest of the party.

"This wind...! Miss Filvis, this is Miss Aiz's wind—her magic!!"

"Don't be ridiculous! How in the world would one person be able to produce wind this strong? That's inconceivable!"

As Lefiya shouted in excitement, cheeks stained red, Filvis blanched next to her.

But that didn't keep the elven duo from heading toward the source of the wind, as well.

"Unbelievable..."

And finally, deep within Knossos, in the Evils' lair.

Barca found himself at a loss for words as he watched the scene playing out in the watery film in front of him.

"Wind? Wind, you say? To think that a single girl could produce this kind of magic...turning the tables on not only our thousand-year ambition...but our ancestor's great masterpiece itself."

There was a limit to the orichalcum doors, after all. Rarer by far than the adamantite, the material had been installed only at key points throughout the labyrinth, meaning it would be impossible for him to completely shut off the river of wind winding from tunnel to tunnel, staircase to staircase, as it circumvented the entire maze.

"Everything will be...undone."

The Daedalus of old had upheld a certain aesthetic.

An art in the chaos that made up the maze. By embedding a single light of order into the midst of its lawlessness, one could reveal its inner beauty. It was a principle that Barca and the rest of the great architect's descendants followed even now, never straying from the master blueprints as they strove to complete his masterpiece.

Which was why, much like a certain other Dungeon, Knossos had hidden within it a main route. An "ariadne guide," to put it another way.

And no matter how many of the orichalcum doors Barca shut, that main route would still exist, effusing that girl's wind and leading her companions straight to her.

"Will they assemble around her, then...? With their dying breath?"

They were certainly keeping an incredible pace. Staggeringly so.

And as they all converged on the same location, Barca was unable to stop them. Try as he might to shut the doors in their path, he couldn't even slow them down—Tiona and her group slid under every door just in time, and Gareth effortlessly blocked their descent with his great arms. Everything he tried proved to be too little, too late in the face of their whirlwind speed. There were even some doors he wasn't able to shut at all, thanks to the violas and other monsters of the maze reacting to the wind and amassing in the tunnels, which made it impossible to close them off. He simply wasn't able to get them in his grasp.

The single source of wind had breathed life back into the half-dead adventurers.

It was proof of the girl's faith in her companions.

"They were supposed to be separated..."

Unbelievable. The word passed his lips again.

"This is the true power of *Loki Familia*..." he murmured as both his real eye and the eye bearing a *D* hidden beneath his bangs widened. "...The true power of the Sword Princess."

The roar of the girl's furious squall sent a shiver through his body.

And now, back in the present.

"Hey."

Levis whirled around at the sound of the footsteps behind her.

There was a swath of gray fur parting the darkness of one of the room's many exits.

"—Freak of nature."

It was Bete, the first of *Loki Familia*'s adventurers to reach the source of the wind.

Taking in the sight of Aiz in front of him, bloodied and bruised and about to be cut down by Levis, his fur bristled. His face tattoo twisting in rage, the werewolf bared his teeth with a savage curl of his lip.

"Go to hell!!"

"You're that werewolf…!"

Levis cursed under her breath, readying her counterattack as Bete made a beeline directly toward her.

Neither one of them wanted to give up the first strike.

But it was Levis who misread the attack.

"_____"

She may have feasted on magic stones, but she wasn't the only one who'd grown in power since their fight in the pantry—Bete, too, had gained a level and was now a Level 6.

And his fangs had already sunk into Aiz's wind.

"Ruuuuuuuuuoooooooooooooaaaagggggggggghhhhhhhhhhhhhh!!"

"?!"

In a flash, his Frosvirt became imbued with the gale.

The new speed and power behind his metal boots surpassed anything Levis could have expected, and the sword she'd raised in her counteroffensive was knocked from her hands.

It was an opening, and new shadows had already gathered around the creature woman to take advantage of the gap in her defenses.

"Having fun bullying our sister, are ya?"

"An Amazon…?!"

Immediately after Bete, Tione leaped forward like a snake, flourishing her twin Kukri knives. In a flurry of repeated flashes, she drew a shower of blood from Levis's body, sending the red-haired creature crumbling to the ground.

But the wave of attacks didn't end there.

"——We ain't gonna go easy on ya!"

Directly overhead, the Amazon's other half came flying toward her with her oversize weapon, her normal smile gone at the sight of Aiz's wounds. Now, nothing but pure, unadulterated rage burned in Tiona's eyes, and Levis was unable to do anything but stare in shock as the double-bladed Urga came at her at full power.

"Take *this*————!!"

"Guurraaagh!!"

The monster sword cleaved through Levis's longsword—and her arm with it. Her forearm went spinning through the air, cut cleanly from the elbow.

"_____"

Before Levis even had a chance to recover, all she could see was a rocklike fist sailing straight toward her face.

"Off ye go now."

It was Gareth.

"Gunnghh?!"

The punch passed easily over the arm she'd brought up to try and defend herself, driving into her frame and sending her flying through the air with the force of a raging river. When she slammed into the far wall, a mushroom-like cloud of dirt and dust erupted from the impact, and the hall shook around them.

The battle over, *Loki Familia*'s first-tier adventurers lowered their weapons and raced toward Aiz.

"Aiz!"

"Are you all right?!"

"Like hell she's all right! Goddamn, you Amazons are as blind as you are dumb!"

"Tiona...Tione...Mister Bete..." Aiz murmured, a smile making its way to her face at the sight of her companions, who had been guided to her by her wind. She accepted the potion they scrambled to push on her with a grateful "Thank you..."

"As much as I'd like t'scold ye...ye did well, lass."

"It...wasn't me. It was...thanks to all of you..."

Aiz could only shake her head at Gareth's unexaggerated praise. But even as they sat there, countless footsteps could already be heard approaching the room.

"Mister Gareth! There you guys are!"

"Raul! Is—is that the captain?! What in the gods' holy names happened here?!"

"Keep it together, Tione!"

First Raul and Aki appeared, carrying with them the wounded Finn, and Tione flew into a panic far unlike any produced by the labyrinth's perils. A moment later, Rakuta, Elfie, and the rest of Bete's and Tiona's groups followed, all filtering into the room one after another.

"Gramps! Finn's gotten himself cursed! Looks bad, too!"

"Aye, I know it, I know it! And what about you lot? What kinda state are ye in?"

"Arcus and I've been poisoned! Got attacked by some poison vermis!"

"Lefiya, Leene, and the others still haven't made it!"

Amid the rapid-fire updates, Gareth quickly began dishing out orders, and *Loki Familia* responded with a practiced celerity. Carrying out the emergency measures with the same precision they'd had on so many of their expeditions, the reunited familia members got straight to work.

"...What are those incompetent fools in *Thanatos Familia* doing?"

"!"

They all turned around to see Levis rising from the cloud of dust. Though battered by *Loki Familia*'s earlier attacks, her murderous ardor had yet to wane.

"No bother, though. I'll take out these vermin myself...here and now."

"...You and what army?" Tione smirked, ready with her Kukri knives, Zolas, as the red-haired creature woman began exuding an incomparable sense of presence and malice.

Levis, however, merely narrowed her eyes coldly in the face of the ten-plus adventurers. "It would be a simple task to eliminate you as you are now. But I'll call in that army if you wish."

Poison vermis lesions, skill-induced fatigue, an arm crushed by a door—they certainly weren't in any condition to fight, and realizing Levis had seen their exhaustion, Tiona, Bete, and the others closed their mouths as sweat dribbled down their temples. Even now, their items had almost been entirely used up, meaning they'd have no way to heal the injuries Knossos had given them.

Levis began consuming magic power to repair her wounded body as she pressed her severed arm against the bloody stump of her elbow. It connected itself at once, restoring life to her fist and palm as though it hadn't just been lying on the floor, and Raul and the other lower-level familia members gulped.

"...A spare ax, lass. Toss it to me," Gareth hissed to one of the supporters.

"R-right!"

The dwarven soldier, equipped with half-shattered armor and sporting considerable injuries, accepted the offered weapon, preparing himself for battle.

Aiz, too, readied her sword, looking directly at Levis.

Just then.

The walls of the room—*came crashing to the ground.*

"Huh?!"

It happened without warning.

A swath of steely skin suddenly obscured a side of their vision.

And as the great hulking beast lumbered toward them in a shower of stone and adamantite, none of them could breathe.

Even Levis looked surprised. But it was Gareth who found his voice first, shouting at the top of his lungs.

"RUUUUUUUUUUUUUUUUUUNNNN!!"

And they did, abandoning everything and retreating from the room.

They flew toward the exit en masse. And as for the lower-ranked members who couldn't get to their feet as quickly, Aiz, Tiona, Tione, Bete, Raul, and the other higher-ranked adventurers grabbed them by their clothes and yanked them along for the ride.

"How did Gugalanna get here of all places? Shit...!"

Levis revealed that this was an Irregular for them, as well, before disappearing inside the dilapidated labyrinth wall.

Aiz watched her go, but that was all she could do, because the giant creature now blocking their vision was hot on *Loki Familia*'s heels.

"What's going on, what's going on, *what's going on*?! What the hell is that thing?!"

"How the hell am I supposed to know?!"

Bete answered Tiona's bewilderment with an angry shout as the raging destruction around them swallowed up the tunnel. Clueless as to what was going on, all they could do was run into another large room up ahead.

An earthquake-size explosion rent the air behind them.

"_____?!"

The shock hit their backs, sending them flying.

They tumbled across the ground, lower-levels and elites alike, somehow getting up to turn around…just as a colossal silhouette emerged from the shadows.

Four impossibly large, powerful legs supported its lower half, two mangled horns twisted away from its head, and its skin was the sickly yellowish-green of corroded steel. It was tall, more than six meders from the ground to its shoulders, and from its back sprouted a tail that split in two down the middle, both ends sharpened into swordlike points.

All in all, it very much resembled an ox, save for one thing—the woman's body jutting out from the creature's forehead. The upper half of its body was female, its lips curved in a disconcerting smile.

"Did it just…break through the adamantite walls—like it was nothing…?!" Raul murmured in horrified awe as the first-tier adventurers felt an unsettling sense of déjà vu wash over them.

And then, as though summoning the nightmare back to reality, Aiz said its name.

"A demi-spirit…!"

CHAPTER 5

BATTLE OF TEARS

Гэта казка іншага сям'і.

Гнеў / Wailing / Татальная вайна

A short while before *Loki Familia* reunited with Aiz.

"—Things have taken quite the interesting twist, I see."

Thanatos turned toward the new voice, still in the mural-lined room Lefiya and Filvis had left not long ago, and confirmed its owner.

"Ishtar…yes?"

Her copper skin was laid bare to reveal much of her ample chest and supple limbs, and she was every bit the renowned enchantress who'd stolen the glances of so many. Kiseru pipe in hand, the Goddess of Beauty Ishtar narrowed her eyes in Thanatos's direction.

"And what a surprise this is, my *dear* sponsor. Welcome to the grand halls of Knossos!…Or so I'd like to say, but you don't seem in the mood for pleasantries, hmm? Coming here of your own volition as you have."

"A little too late for that, isn't it? Just how many times do you think I've been to this rat's nest now? You're a difficult god to find, do you know that? We've been looking for some time," Ishtar replied, clearly no stranger to Knossos's tunnels. Behind her stood one of her human followers, as well as their masked guide.

The two familias, *Ishtar Familia* and the Evils' Remnants, were closely entwined. Though to be truthful, *Ishtar Familia* consisted of no one but Ishtar and a few others.

The completion of Knossos required considerable materials and funds, something that the Evils—Barca and the other Daedalus descendants included—didn't have. This was why they'd forged their contract with Njǫrðr to benefit from Meren's black-market dealings.

But that was only one of their plans, and their dealings with Ishtar were another. What with the brothels of Orario's Pleasure Quarter under her command, Ishtar's familia possessed easily the greatest source of funds in all of Orario, at least after Orario's largest and second-largest familias—Loki's and Freya's, respectively. Unlike the high-risk, high-return Dungeon familias, she incurred almost no costs or losses, making it more of a no-risk, high-return venture and the source of her power.

"Well, you've found me! And for what purpose, may I ask?"

After all, Ishtar wasn't helping the Evils for the hell of it. She wanted something in return, as well.

Namely—

"The Bull of Heaven I'm to receive. I would like to see its power."

—the powerful being the Evils and the creatures were hiding.

"The time has almost come for me to have my revenge on Freya. Once I've gotten my hands on that rabbit, my bait, I'll need to strike within only a few days' time. I may need to lure her brats here...and before that happens, I want to be completely sure of its strength."

"...Erm, well..."

As a wicked grin unbefitting a Goddess of Beauty crossed Ishtar's face, Thanatos started hemming and hawing.

"You are aware of what's going on in your own labyrinth, aren't you? You know that *Loki Familia* is wandering its halls? I can think of no better opportunity to test its strength."

"It's just...You know, Ishtar? *Loki Familia* doesn't even have a key. They're just about done as it is, even without pulling the age-old final boss to bring them down. Quite the opposite, in fact, it would only create more chaos for us..." Thanatos tried to explain.

"Like I care about any of that," Ishtar answered curtly. "Just how much money do you think I've showered you with these past five years, hmm?"

"Fine, fine..." Thanatos put up his hands in defeat as she removed her kiseru pipe from between her lips and let out a puff of purple smoke. "I get it. I'll do it. Anything for my dear sponsor."

"Good." Ishtar narrowed her eyes in apparent satisfaction before turning on her heel. "Take me somewhere where I'll be able to watch." She and her attendant made their way back and out of the hall, followed shortly by the masked figure.

Watching this, one of Thanatos's followers came up beside him. "Wh-what should we do, Lord Thanatos? That creature woman gave us strict orders not to use it yet..."

"Guess we're stuck between a rock and a hard place. Ishtar's been good to us, after all. If we upset her now, who knows what'll happen."

Remembering the beautiful goddess's fickle temper, Thanatos replied with a shrug before slowly smiling.

"And honestly—I kinda wanna see it, too. Just how strong is this trump card of Enyo's, I wonder?"

The robed follower shuddered and gulped at the god's dark smile.

Thus his acolytes set about their task in a flurry of activity.

Releasing the monster from the chains that bound it.

"You fools! Is this nothing but a game to you...?!" Levis shouted indignantly from the pile of rubble.

One corner of the room had been completely inundated with the broken remains of the maze wall. Piles upon piles of stone and adamantite lay strewn about, completely blocking off the way to Aiz and her companions.

It didn't take long for Levis to realize it was Thanatos and his crew who had released the monster, and the revelation brought with it considerable exasperation.

"My voice isn't reaching it...Is Aria's wind blocking it?" Levis extended a hand in the direction the monster had chased Aiz's group before clenching into a fist. "If this keeps up, then the others, too...Dammit. I'll need to check on them."

With that, she put the room behind her.

"Don't go getting devoured on me, Aria...It will make retrieving your body...*difficult*."

"Miss Filvis, what was that noise just now...?"

"...I don't know. But it sounded close."

Lefiya and Filvis were running down the labyrinth's tunnels

themselves. Though they'd lost their guide when Aiz's wind had come to an abrupt stop, this new sound farther down the passage spurred them on in another direction.

It didn't take them long to reach the end of the hall, and soon their companions, including a certain golden-haired, golden-eyed swordswoman, entered their field of vision.

"Miss Aiz!" Lefiya called out, bubbling up with relief and joy. But her solace soon changed to suspicion when not one of her companions turned around at their approach.

Her doubt lasted no more than a few seconds.

Because as she followed everyone's line of sight, she saw the sinister monstrosity of a creature that had captured her companions' attention, and she came to a stop herself.

"Th-that thing…Is it the same as the…fifty-ninth floor…?!"

Protruding from the forehead of the colossal ox was a decidedly female-shaped form; its small, two-meder stature contrasted oddly with the behemoth below.

Its short emerald hair and similarly green skin, its richly colored dress, and the eerie smile on features beautiful enough for a goddess turned the sea of Lefiya's memories into a storm.

It was a demi-spirit, the same as the one they'd desperately fought against in the Unknown Frontier of the fifty-ninth floor.

"——*Aaaahh.*"

It was then that the demi-spirit moved.

It was also when Lefiya realized she'd chosen a terribly unfortunate time to reconvene with her companions.

Without any explanation, the creature entered full attack mode.

"————————————*Nnn!*"

It started with a simple attack.

But that simple attack brought with it unimaginable weight and destructive power.

Aiz and the others quickly jumped out of the way, evading it with every bit of speed and strength they had left, but the spirit merely gave chase with little regard for the devastation it was wreaking on the labyrinth walls in its rampage.

"N-no way!"

"It's ripping through the adamantite like paper...!"

As Lefiya yelped in shock, Filvis responded with similar awe. The rest of the group landed right next to the two elves' feet at that moment, in an equal state of stunned silence. Not even Gareth, confident as he was in his strength, could make a dent in those walls without considerable time and effort, and in a single swing of its limbs, this thing was felling the massive adamantite barriers like they were nothing but building blocks.

Not a single member of *Loki Familia* uttered a sound as they stared at the gaping new hole in the maze's walls.

"...'Tis a different beast from what we found on the fifty-ninth floor—built for sheer power," Gareth murmured as he readjusted his helm.

Each one of its powerful strikes was a veritable killing blow, making the beast a power type, through and through.

"What's the plan here, huh? Fight that thing? Or get the hell outta here?" Bete hissed.

"You even have to ask?! We run! The captain needs to be healed, pronto!" Tione snarled back.

"Yeah, but you know that thing's just gonna follow us, right?" Tiona interjected, uncharacteristically subdued.

"...I'll act as bait."

"Oh no you *won't!*"

Aiz started to offer an idea, but Tiona immediately shot it down.

In front of the smoking hole in front of them, they saw the giant outline of the beast slowly retreat from the room. Sweat ran down their temples.

"We still don't even know the way to the exit..." Raul muttered, face pale.

"Yeah, and if that thing keeps up its rampage, it might even destroy our only way out...Ha-ha...ha-ha-ha..." Narfi added with a dull laugh.

"I'm sorry, but I'll have to pass on being buried alive!" Aki affirmed, pressing at the wounds on her arms with a grimace.

Seeing the hope dwindling in her companions, Lefiya leaned forward. "I—I have found the exit! I can guide you there!"

That was when the other familia members finally noticed her and looked in her direction. A moment later, she was greeted with a chorus of *heys*. Among them, Tione's "You're the bomb, Lefiya!!" was particularly prominent.

"Then all we've got left is that great big thing over there..." Raul posed, and as if on cue, the demi-spirit in question reappeared in the room. Ever so slowly, it turned around, the bovine eyes of its lower half and crescent-shaped eyes of its female upper half both falling on Aiz and the rest of the group.

They needed to make a decision.

A single strong voice to tell them what to do. Or perhaps a choice that didn't shy away from sacrifices.

Second by second, their precious time began to tick away.

And at long last, the uncertain eyes of everyone in the group settled on one individual.

Their prum captain, currently hoisted on the back of one of their female members.

"...Ngh."

Near death, Finn scrunched up his face.

Had the loss of blood muddled his thoughts? Or was even Finn Deimne, of all people, hesitating to relay the necessary order?

In that moment of their commander's indecision—another voice rang true.

"Let it out, Finn."

It was Gareth.

"Woulda been commonplace but a short time ago," the dwarf continued, readying his ax as he took his place beside Finn. "Who is it who's always been the one to cover yer arses, aye?" His lips turned up in a smile beneath his beard.

The expression brought the inklings of a grin to Finn's lips, as well.

"...I leave the back line in...your capable hands, Gareth."

"Roger that!"

And with one final ferocious grin, Gareth was racing toward the colossal fiend at breakneck speed. As all eyes followed his departure, Raul, too, frowned at the sight of the dwarf's shrinking back—before issuing a command of his own in place of Finn:

"All troops—*retreat*! Get the hell out of here! Lefiya, you're in the lead!"

"R-roger!...Miss Filvis!"

"...Right. Let's go."

Loki Familia was off in a flash. With Lefiya and Filvis taking point, the whole group sprinted toward the nearest tunnel.

However, it was then that the previously silent Amazonian twins turned toward their companions.

"...Like hell I'm gonna let Gareth be the only cool one. Gotta earn my praise from the captain, after all!"

"Me neither! Me neither!"

The two belligerent twins ran off after the lone dwarf. Neither one was known for following orders, and they weren't going to leave Gareth behind.

"Bete, Aiz...you need to...protect everyone else..."

"...Hmph!"

The werewolf's tail had begun to wag in anticipation of following them, but at Finn's orders, Bete simply grunted disapprovingly. Both he and Aiz gave Gareth and the two sisters one last look as they made their way out of the room.

"Tiona, Tione...Gareth..." Aiz murmured.

Don't lose.

Heartbroken, entrusting the fate of the party to her friends at the rear, Aiz fled.

"Is it really all right, Tione? Leavin' Finn's side an' all?" Gareth asked as the two Amazons ran to join him.

"If anyone's gonna be looking after the captain's rear, it's me! That's who it belongs to, after all!"

"Since when did this become about butts?"

At Tione's indignant shout, Tiona looked on in half-lidded incredulity. It could very well be the last time they would be able to crack jokes in that one-hundred-meder-square room as they held their weapons—ax, Kukri knives, and Urga, respectively—at the ready.

"...*Aaahh*."

But the jokes stopped there.

In front of them, the titanic mammoth moved.

KA-PHWOOM. The dull crack thundered around them like someone had just smacked the earth with a giant hammer—the thing had taken a step forward. And it was headed straight for the tunnel where Aiz and the rest of the group had just departed.

"What do we do, then, huh?" Tiona posed, her skin still slick with sweat from the poison vermis toxins.

"Well, it's certainly not an enemy we can take head-on, especially in our condition..." Tione replied, still inflicted herself with wounds from the assassins' cursed weapons. Though the cuts were light, they wouldn't heal. "We should aim at its magic stone. Try to take it out in a single hit."

It had taken a full party and considerable time to defeat the demi-spirit last time. With only three of them now, and at less than optimal strength, they were going to have some trouble holding this thing back.

"Aye, that'll work...but let's consider the basics for a moment, hmm? What's the theory on givin' big lugs what for, lassies?"

"Aim for the feet."

"Drop it to the ground!"

"Let's get on with it, then! One hit to blow that beastie to kingdom come! And don't let it hit ye, either!"

In spite of everything, the adventurers were not to be daunted, for they knew all too well that pessimism was the worst toxin of all.

Gareth raised his ax, still in his half-charred armor from the earlier wave of flames. "Give everything ye got to stop that thing's feet! No lettin' it get to our chums now. Off we go!"

With that, the dwarf kicked off the ground, the signal for the battle to start.

"It gets away from us and we've already lost! Tiona, stop it in its tracks!"

"Roger that!"

"And Tione—you use yer magic to bind its legs!"

"Magic's not exactly my strong suit, but...I'll do what I can do!"

Gareth and Tiona ran straight at the creature, as Tione leaped off to the side, momentarily distancing herself from the battle proper. Immediately, she began casting a spell.

"*Aria...Aria!*"

The demi-spirit, on the other hand, went into a maddened rush, crying out in excited fervor. Its feet thundered toward them along the stone-covered adamantite floor and created tremors that echoed up and throughout the entire maze.

""Ngh!!""

Gareth and Tiona quickly split to the left and right, dodging the incoming bull.

But the creature itself wasn't the only thing they had to worry about—its charge created massive blasts of air that pummeled their bodies as they raced past.

"It's...pretty fast when it wants to be!"

"Yer tellin' me!"

The two had fallen with their hands to the stone floor because of the vibration. The demi-spirit, meanwhile, simply continued on toward the exit.

Once that thing started running, there was no way they could stop it.

Watching the enormous bull's mad dash, Gareth let out a howl.

"Tione! It's makin' to leave!"

Across the room, the Amazon was weaving her song.

"*Desire, submersed in the sea of my heart; thirst, borne from the seas of my heart—the time has come,*" she chanted, carefully forming the less familiar spell so as not to miss a syllable.

She had never studied the ways of the mage, so no magic circle formed beneath her feet to accompany her powerful incantation echoing off the walls. She turned her attention to the demi-spirit racing across her field of vision, assuming a battle stance. *"Take shape, bare your fangs, and become the serpent. Free yourself of the sea, cross the rising knolls, and engulf the world. Time is yours for the taking. Halt fate's ticking seconds, and banish it to the void!"*

A glimmering light materialized in Tione's hand as she completed the spell, magic taking shape in the form of a bluish-purple whip of light.

"Restrict Iorum!"

It flew straight at the beast.

It struck with the speed of a snake, a predator devouring its prey, and wrapped itself firmly around the bull's right hind leg.

"?!"

Almost immediately, the demi-spirit's body stiffened.

"Holy cow! I got it!"

Tione's spell, Restrict Iorum.

As a restrictive magic that bound its victims in a whip of light, it had a set chance of rooting enemies to the spot. Its whip could even be used as an ordinary weapon if the necessity arose, and its hit rate was dependent on Tione's magic stat. Not being a mage, Tione had never trained her magic, but her high level made for a high magic power all the same. In her own words, it would probably hit "one for ten on a floor boss."

Celebrating her good luck at having pulled off a hit on her first try, Tione took control of the whiplike reins.

"Hngh...?"

The restrained demi-spirit pushed against the powerful inertia holding its body.

The female upper half was shocked to find itself at a halt against its will, and as the bovine lower half pitched forward, its powerful front legs dug into the ground to keep itself from falling over.

It created an opening that the other first-tier adventurers didn't miss.

"Huurraaagh!!"

"Hwuogh!!"

Tiona and Gareth veered toward the creature's backside, tearing into its legs.

"Th-this thing's hard as a rock! What the hell? It cracked my Urga!"

Each adventurer had taken one of the beast's hind legs, but the assault rewarded them with nothing but shock. Just as Tiona had so boisterously shouted, a clean crack had formed in her Urga, and the blade of Gareth's ax was now missing a sizable chunk.

Not only was the spirit's skin remarkably thick, it boasted a granitic solidity easily as strong as adamantite's.

"*That hurts.*"

But Tiona and Gareth weren't the two strongest warriors of *Loki Familia* for nothing.

And despite their own casualties, their blows had left wounds in the brute's rigid skin that were now gushing blood.

"Like as not, our weapons'll knuckle under before us!"

"Whatcha think we should do, then?"

"The only thing we can—smash it while we've weapons left to smash with!"

The two kicked off the floor for a second lunge at the spirit. In a violent flurry of heated blows, they lambasted the thing's legs again and again.

"...*You want to play with me?*" The spirit's languid golden eyes turned toward them. It cocked its head to the side with a laugh, almost like an elephant observing a swarm of mice. "*Then—let's play.*"

In a flash, it pulled itself free of Tione's binding whip, turning its hulking body to face Gareth and Tiona head-on.

"A-already...?!" Tione lamented. The spirit's magic power was simply too great, allowing it to break through her restraints in the blink of an eye. Hoping to halt the thing's movements for even a moment more, Tione yanked back on her whip—

But then.

"Ngh?!"

It was Tione who ended up getting pulled forward when the bull stomped its leg with such force that it sent her tumbling to the floor.

"Oh sh—!"

The thunderous crack shook the very walls.

The mice managed to escape the elephant, but the tromp of its mighty foot still sent them flying.

And the adamantite floor was once again split, a smoking pile of rubble.

"Ha-ha...HA-HA-HA-HA-HA-HA!"

The nightmarish rodeo had begun.

Stomping and spinning, it moved. That was it. And that was all it had to do to have the battle-hardened first-tier adventurers reeling. The earthquakes it created sent them to their knees, and the shock waves from its footsteps pummeled the dwarf's armor and the Amazons' copper skin. Even the spirit's forked tail contributed to the punishing onslaught, flailing from its hindquarters like a bladed whip.

"Huuuuuaaaaaaarrrrrrrrrrrgggh!" The maddened bull gave a great roar that joined with the sweetly sadistic laughter of its upper half. Its two entities bearing their own separate desires and inclinations, the demi-spirit rampaged, attacking not only its prey but the labyrinth itself.

"An absolute frenzy if I've ever seen one...! Ye don't think it was a power bull that thing parasitized, do ye?"

"Never seen one that big before! This thing's crazy!"

Unable to withstand the onslaught any further, Gareth and Tiona put distance between themselves and the beast. Tione, meanwhile, was furiously attempting to pull her whip back in her direction, though her efforts were currently going unrewarded.

The creature's body itself, seemingly limitless in its potential, was proving to be its best weapon.

"Seems our choice has been made for us, aye? We shatter that stone!" Gareth shouted, already preparing for the monumental task.

"This goddamn cow...!" And with that, Tione flew into an *all-out frenzy.* Unable to take the way the spirit was flinging her around however it pleased, she completely ignored Gareth's suggestion in favor of attack mode. She didn't even release the grip of her Restrict Iorum from the spirit's leg; instead, she swung in a wide circle around the demi-spirit, using its body as a fulcrum.

"?" The demi-spirit glanced down curiously at the whip now encircling all four of its legs, though this new development didn't seem to hinder its spree of destruction.

Tione, on the other hand, was moving at an incredible speed, launching herself forward and off the ground as she came flying toward the beast—and the center of her circle—with the force of a whirlwind.

"You're gonna stop all that racket—before I *make* you!!"

"?!"

The furious iron fist she slammed into the spirit's body was not only backed by an enormous centrifugal force but further strengthened by her Berserk skill. And after a resounding *thud*, even though Tione's every finger was shattered upon impact, the sheer power behind the strike was enough to send the beast to its knees. It had "hit the spot" in every sense of the phrase.

"Atta girl, lass!" Gareth called out as he and Tiona started at once for the stalled demi-spirit. They pelted the beast's wounded limbs, paying no heed to the flying chips and pieces of their weapons. And when the spirit lashed out with its tail, Gareth simply severed the forked appendage with his ax, to its stunned dismay.

"...*Pierce, spear of lightning! Your envoy beseeches thee, Tonitrus! Incarnate of thunder! Queen of lightning—!*"

As the bull's movements had weakened, its female upper half had suddenly stopped smiling, and the short chant, even shorter and faster than humans could possibly imagine, was complete in an instant.

"*THUNDER RAY!*"

A magic circle sparked to life in midair, and the spirit thrust its arm in the direction of its incoming assailant—Tiona, flying directly toward its side.

"Show me somethin' new already!"

But Tiona leaped swiftly over the electrifying magic barrage almost as though she'd been expecting it. She was already well acquainted with the lance of lightning from their battle on the fifty-ninth floor, and sticking her tongue out at it now as she flew past, she continued in her course toward the creature's body, swiping her Urga up and through it as she slid between its legs. Its blade sliced clean through the knee of its already heavily damaged hind leg.

"_____?!"

The bull let out a moan of agony, giant globules of spittle flying from its lips, and as it bucked, its upper half joined it with a scream at the unwelcome turn of events.

—Its charges and attacks were a threat to be reckoned with, to be sure. From the perspective of a wall like Gareth, whose duty it was to protect the mages and the rest of the group from its unstoppable advances, it made for nothing short of a nightmare. But that was it.

This was a power-type demi-spirit, unlike the magic-type they'd crossed swords with on the fifty-ninth floor. While its overwhelming destructive power and unadulterated defensive strength were truly awe-inspiring, that was all it had.

It was, quite honestly, boring.

For *Loki Familia* especially, who'd challenged the unknown of the Dungeon's depths a hundred times over on their many expeditions, this new enemy before them now was practically docile. Compared to the tentacle-wielding, flower petal–armored demi-spirit they'd taken down on the fifty-ninth floor, this raging bull was entirely more manageable. Its potential was staggering, enough to offset its maladroit attacks, but even as the trio was knocked off their feet, their skin littered with cuts and bruises and blood flowing freely from fresh wounds, they continued all the same, weapons never stopping.

"Huuuuurrrrrrraaaaaaaaaaaaggghhh!!"

The back line had been left in their capable hands, and their spirit, tenacity, and hearts—constantly focused on their companions up ahead—drove them in their back-and-forth dance of attack and defense.

It was a ferocious contest of endurance, and none of them knew which would fall first—their minds, bodies, and weapons or the creature's legs. And as the spirit launched a desperate defense of its magic-stone core with what was left of its tail and magic, its upper half—the spirit's face—grew noticeably harried.

"...!"

It was the demi-spirit that came out on the bottom of the duel.

The last of its tail completely severed, its bovine lower half finally sunk completely to its knees with an earth-shattering rumble.

"Gotcha!"

"Burn in hell, you cow!"

First Tiona, then Tione, then Gareth leaped at the spirit's upper half, coming at it from three different directions in synchronized coordination. Even if the spirit tried to attack one of them with its magic, the other two would have no problem reaching and smashing its magic-stone core. And that was if the thing even had time to cast one of its short spells to begin with.

At once, the double-bladed sword, Kukri knives, and giant ax descended upon the spirit's body.

"—Aha."

But just then.

Sailing toward the spirit's front, Gareth saw it—the odiously pure smile gracing its face.

"*Rage, fury of the skies.*"

In that single stanza.

The magic was invoked.

"*Caelum Veil.*"

A *short-chant spell.*

In the single instant it took the magic to bloom, time seemed to come to a screeching halt.

What formed was a membrane-like film of uncountable bolts of lightning. It surrounded the spirit like electro-charged armor, protecting both its lower and upper halves from attack.

—An enchantment.

Just like Aiz's Airiel.

The already ridiculously powerful monster had just proven itself again, this time with the almighty blessing of the sky's fury. It was the being's trump card, and with this final hand, the puerile smile on its face changed to one of amused chicanery.

"Distel."

In the next instant, lightning struck.

"——?!"

The electrically charged waves surrounding its body shot out in every direction. Trapped in the deadly web of high-voltage currents, Gareth and the others could do nothing but scream in noiseless agony before their bodies were flung through the air in identical arcs. They landed hard on their backs, bodies seared from head to toe.

"——Ahhhh."

But the real finishing blow had yet to come.

Glimmering gold particles gathering around its battered limbs, the spirit began to restore itself and rose once more to its feet. The current of electricity crackled all the way to its horns as the mighty bull reared up with its head toward the ceiling.

And in its shadow lay the three battered adventurers.

—It couldn't possibly be.

But it was; its descending hooves spelling almost certain death to Gareth, Tiona, and Tione on the ground.

With a final sadistic smile, its legs came down and, with them, the web of high-voltage current.

"Ruuuuaaaaaaaaaarrrrrrrrrrrrrrrggggggggggggggggggghhhhhhhhhh!"

The blast was catastrophic.

When the hooves of thunder slammed down into the middle of the room, innumerous shock waves and rippling tremors of electricity assailed the entire perimeter. The wave of high-voltage destruction consumed not only Gareth and the others still on the ground but the entirety of the room itself—the floor, the walls, the ceiling—destroying everything in its path.

The sound was deafening, and their world was painted a brilliant, sizzling white.

Deep cracks formed along the surrounding surfaces, the metal underneath curving and threatening to give at a moment's notice. The only thing that kept the floor from collapsing beneath them was the layers upon layers of adamantite covering—and its builders' millennia of deep-rooted delusions.

"Aha—aha-ha-ha-ha-ha-ha-ha-ha-ha-ha-ha-ha!!"

The spirit's laughter echoed throughout the cavern as the walls of Knossos came down around it.

"Ha-ha-ha-ha-ha-ha-ha-ha-ha-ha-ha-ha-ha-ha-ha-ha-ha-ha-ha!!"

Ishtar's gleeful mirth echoed that of the spirit's as she watched its destruction unfold from the watery film atop the maze's pedestal.

"How wonderfully droll!! Look at the way it plays with Loki's brats! Like they're nothing more than ants! Look, Tammuz! It makes even the floor bosses look like mere playthings!" she cried, like a whore about to climax, to the noiseless young man next to her. Her cheeks were flushed red with excitement at the overwhelming power of the beast in the images.

And now its potential had risen even higher thanks to its enchantment of thunder.

Its enhanced strength, specialized for both offense and defense, was nothing short of heinous.

The Bull of Heaven was truly in a league all its own.

"This will take down Freya!! This is all I need to slaughter her brats right in front of her eyes! I win, Freya! I win!! Ha-ha...*ha-ha-ha-ha-ha-ha-ha-ha-ha-ha*!!" she cackled, practically bent backward in her maniacal laughter.

Meanwhile, Thanatos was having trouble keeping the sneer off his face, a short ways away from Ishtar as he watched her revelry.

"A spectacular display. Frighteningly so. To think you were hiding such a titan, Levis dear," he murmured to the absent creature woman, lips turning upward in their typical scythe-like smile.

"L-Lord Thanatos! The destruction has sent Lord Barca into a fit…! We can't calm him down! At this rate, the Sword Princess will get away!"

"Please, you must get him under control!"

"What's that? I don't hear anything!" Thanatos merely replied, feigning deafness to their cries even as his beaten and battered followers raced into the stone chamber. Turning away from them and their inconvenient truth, he looked, instead, to the scene playing out in the watery film.

"If only we'd had this creature back then…" he continued, eyes narrowing at the sight of that towering demi-spirit as he thought back to their defeat five years ago.

All was still.

Surrounded by the piles of rubble and debris, the now-quiet demi-spirit began to move. *Thwoom…thwoom…*Its giant feet thudded one after another toward the tunnel Aiz and the others had disappeared down not long ago.

"?"

Sensing something wrapped around it, the spirit's upper half glanced down at its feet.

That same whip of light from before was still wreathed around its hind leg. Lifting its gaze to the whip's source, it saw Tione directly beside it, having summoned her magic again.

Even though her charred body was heavily wounded after the electric attack.

"You think I'm…just gonna let you…go…?" she hissed, practically doubled over.

The spirit, however, just smiled at the girl and her Restrict Iorum. In the next instant, it flung out its leg to yank the whip as if it were the line on a fishing rod.

The Amazon was powerless to resist, flying along with it and smashing with a painful *thud* into the nearby wall.

"Gnnnaaagh…!!"

"*He-he-he…AHA-HA-HA.*"

Again, its leg lashed out. Again and again.

It flung her every which way, each rumbling shift of its body sending her to the hard surfaces of the ground, the wall, the piles of rubble. And yet, no matter how many times it bashed the girl into the stone, the toy seemed indestructible. *Oh my, how interesting*, it seemed to laugh, tittering like an amused child. That ever-present smile of purity, or perhaps sadism, remained on its lips.

It was nothing but a child, breaking and battering its toys in a game of curious barbarity.

"*Hee-hee…bye-bye.*"

With one last *splat!*

The spirit laughed and turned to leave behind the crumpled body of the girl, her bones crushed and twisted and blood painting the floor.

Another toy awaited. Eagerly calling out to her like a girl in love. Its most prized, precious toy of all—its Aria.

This time, the elephantine creature *would* leave the room behind. But just as it was about to do so…

"…Wa…it…"

"…"

The whip was wrapped around its slender neck now.

And turning only slightly, it saw the girl on her feet once more.

She stood, legs trembling, one of her arms limp and sagging and one of her knees just about having given out. Fresh blood streamed from her forehead, painting her face, and her brows were arched with the desperation of one giving everything she had left.

"If you get out of here…the captain will…He'll…I'll never… never let you…touch him…you pig…" Tears were building up in the corners of her eyes. With the name of her beloved on her lips, she let the incoherent words come tumbling out in heaving sobs.

The demi-spirit frowned, its good feelings gone in an instant.

Would it play with Tione for one last round? But no, it didn't have the intelligence for that. Because from its point of view, Tione was already broken. And it wasn't interested in playing with broken toys.

"I'll protect them…No matter what it takes…to keep you from… getting to them…getting to him…" Her words were slurring now, growing fainter and fainter the more the blood flowed from her body. With one last effort, she gave the whip of light a tug, tightening it ever so slightly around the spirit's neck, but the spirit itself was already done. It wouldn't fight her anymore.

Ignoring her incoherent muttering, it turned on its heels and headed for the exit.

"…?"

When, with a jerk.

The whip around its neck pulled back with a sudden, stronger force.

It made it difficult to breathe, and the spirit turned back again toward the source of the discomfort. The whip of light was pulled taut now. And at its origin stood two figures.

Standing behind the wide-eyed Tione was the dwarven adventurer.

"Ye did well, lass—"

It was Gareth, an indomitable smile on his face, his helm and armor gone and his stout body cut and beaten. He had Tione's whip hand in his, and in his other, he gripped the lash directly.

Eyes glinting, he gave the reins of light a commanding tug.

"—Ye're not goin' anywhere!!"

All of a sudden, the demi-spirit found itself bent backward at a painfully unnatural angle.

"?!"

The whip's coils dug into the green flesh of its neck.

They reeled its body back, back, back until it seemed liable to simply snap off its base. All it could see was the dilapidated ceiling, and its neck gave a disconcerting *creeeeeak* as the whip jerked it further still. Not even its hands, flying up to tear at the tightening coils, could do anything to separate it from its throat.

The whip simply wouldn't give.

Wouldn't allow air through.

Wouldn't allow it to breathe.

Wouldn't allow it to speak.

"Havin' trouble with that beautiful voice, miss? Tryin' to sing one of those songs?—*Aye, try and sing now!!*" Gareth shouted, spraying spit and grinning fiercely.

By crushing the source of the beast's magic, he'd effectively rid it of one of its weapons. And as he put even more power into his great arms and meaty shoulders, the spirit's dull golden eyes widened more than they ever had before.

"Think ye can ignore us, eh? An eyesore of a warrior if I've ever seen one! The moment ye lower yer guard against an adventurer is the moment ye've spelled yer own doom!!"

"...-...-...?!"

"What a disgrace of a spirit we have 'ere, lassies! Can't even speak!!"

The fact that the spirit in his grasp had never been a warrior to begin with was no cause of concern for Gareth. As he put every shred of strength he had into forcing that throat closed, his face turned as red as a tomato. But that didn't stop the groundless taunts from continuing with each creaking snap of the spirit's neck.

And with that same crazed intensity, he shouted to his companion.

"Tione!! Where's that spirit you're so known for, huh?! Don't ye wanna save Finn?!"

The Amazon in front of him pulled an instant one-eighty.

Snapping out of her stupor, her eyes sharpened with a hardened glint. Then, summoning another wave of strength from who knew where, her one good arm snapped back to life.

"Shut up, you walking fossil!! You think I don't know?!"

They were both pulling now, increasing the pressure on the spirit's neck with their almost supernatural strength.

"_____?!"

The spirit gave a noiseless scream.

It didn't know what was happening. Not why it was in such pain, nor why it was receiving this abuse.

Why its toys were *trying to kill it.*

Barely able to think, it struggled against the binding whip, but no matter how it clawed and grappled, the serpent's fangs simply wouldn't let go. The pressure became so intense that tears of blood began streaming down from its eyes.

""HRRRRRRRRUUUAAAAAGGGGGGGGGHHHHHHHH!!""

The adventurers' mighty roars surged up and out of their lungs.

They were attempting to strangle the beast, drawing on a primordial method. Whatever it took, they were going to kill this thing, and as they summoned every last ounce of strength and energy they had left, their throats ripped with bestial cries of furor.

"I'll—I'll protect the captain! I'll protect his ass and cherish it with everything I have! Because I decided long ago that I'd become a lady and live with the captain and his ass forever and ever and ever!"

"Pfft, ha-ha-ha-ha-ha-ha!! Ye plan to marry just his ass, do ye?!"

"*SHUT UP SHUT UP SHUT UP SHUT UP!!* Why are you even here anyway, you annoying old man?! This should be my big romantic moment with the captain! I'm supposed to hold him and kiss him and pamper his cute little ass! Instead, I'm here with this nasty, mangy, grotty old dwarf wringing the neck of some shit-eating, annoying-as-hell lady monster! It's not faaaaaaair!!"

"Ga-ha-ha-ha-ha!! I know I'm more of a stud than yer precious Finn, but don't get too hot and bothered, Tione!!"

"*I'M GONNA KILL YOOOOOOOOOOOOOOUUUUUUUUUU!!*"

"*Fwa-ha-ha-ha-ha-ha-ha-ha-ha-ha-ha-ha-ha-ha-ha-ha-ha!!*"

It was then that Tione and Gareth broke.

They cried and raged and howled in laughter, overflowing with murderous purpose.

But even as the two of them reached their limit and stepped into the unknown, their duty and savagery coming together in gloriously violent harmony, it was the demi-spirit that gave in first. With their brutish strength, the adventurers sent it nearer and nearer to the precipitous cliff of death, and it was powerless to stop them. No matter how its slender arms struggled, the grip of the tightening serpent stayed strong.

The spirit may have wielded strength beyond human comprehension, but that was only within its bovine lower half. Its magic-throwing upper half, on the other hand, was remarkably frail.

"_____?!"

The bull was spasming now, as well, in tandem with the aggrieved writhing of its female appendage. Unable to take it any longer, it began to move, making to throw off Gareth's and Tione's grips.

Just then.

""Tionaaaaaaaaaaaaaaaaaaaaaaaaaa!!""

The two adventurers abruptly howled.

With a sudden crash, the nearby pile of rubble exploded, revealing Tione's other half speeding toward them.

"Was takin' a nap, is all! You big bastard!!" she shouted with a blood-and-phlegm-laced cough.

She was using a combination of her two skills:

Intense Heat and Berserk.

Both at max power.

With one flying swipe of her Urga—a strike more powerful than any she'd inflicted yet—she took out the gawking bull's legs in an explosion of bone.

"Take this, ya big cow————!"

The demi-spirit's right hind leg was severed from its body.

"Huurrrrrraaaaaaaaarrrrrrrggggghhh?!" The bull howled in pain. As its great hulking body sank to the ground, one of the blades of Tiona's Urga ruptured in a shower of knifelike shards. Between the power behind the strike and the tenacity of the bull's skin, the entire thing had simply shattered.

But that still left the double-bladed weapon with one good blade.

"It ain't over yeeeeeeeeeeeet!!" Tiona shrieked, now wielding her Urga like a greatsword and going after the spirit's other legs.

Driven by pure, concentrated power, she hacked at the remaining legs with cleaving blows, becoming a whirlwind of great Berserk-infused slashes.

"————*Gngh?!*"

Almost as though just remembering it still had its Caelum Veil equipped—and perhaps in a slight state of panic, as well—the demi-spirit released the electrifying energy it had built up. The wave of high-voltage shocks was enough to stop Tiona and her sword in their tracks.

But it wasn't enough.

"Gonna need to do better than thaaaaaaaaaaaaaaaaaaaaaaaaaaat!"

"Try again, asshoooooooooooooooooooooooooooooooooooooole!"

Gareth's and Tione's grips never faltered.

No matter what happened, they wouldn't relinquish their hold on the spirit's neck.

Even as the shocks traveled up the length of the whip, they kept the noose tight.

In fact, if anything, the power seemed to grow stronger still as they burned. Red-hot air poured from Tione's mouth, and the veins in Gareth's arms bulged.

Bloody tears were running rivers down the spirit's cheeks now in place of the agonized screams it couldn't produce.

"Lemme join!!" Tiona suggested before tossing away her one-bladed Urga and bounding to her sister's side to assist in their efforts. Clasping her hands directly around the whip of light, she began to tug as if she were hauling in a giant catch of fish.

All kinds of fluids were pouring from the spirit's eyes now. And its face, too, changed from green to black to an unsettling reddish purple.

As if to overpower the shrieks of the lightning scorching their skin, the first-tier adventurers raised a great, piercing cry in unison.

"""*HRRRRRUUUUUUUUAAAAAAAGGGGGGHHHHHH!!*"""

There was a sickening *squelch*.

And in the next instant, the spirit's head was rent from its neck.

Its hands, now devoid of strength, fell limply to its sides as its severed head went tumbling through the air, eyes rolled back in its head. Blood erupted from its neck like a gurgling fountain, and below it, its bovine lower half slumped sluggishly to the floor.

When the whip of light snapped back on them, the three adventurers, too, were sent tumbling to the ground.

"…Haa…haa…!!" the dwarf sputtered, rising slowly to his feet as the two Amazonian sisters remained spent and motionless next to him. Still trying to get his breath under control, he turned his feet toward the enormous body of the demi-spirit, twitching and spasming in pain.

"—It's over."

He was off, sprinting toward the headless, immobile body of his enemy. Snatching up the one-bladed Urga, he launched himself off a nearby pile of rubble into the air.

He came down from on high, directly above the creature's upper half and the wavering geyser of blood—and delivered the finishing blow.

"RETURN TO THE ASHEEEEEEEEEEEEEEEEEEEEEEEEEES!!"

The blast came seconds later.

No sooner had his blade shattered the spirit's magic stone than its gargantuan body mushroomed up in ash. The weapon continued straight through and into the floor underneath, splitting it into giant chunks of stone.

Around him, the ash settled into a fine mist that permeated the air.

And by the time the echoes of the final strike faded into silence, a lone figure was emerging from the fog.

The old dwarven soldier approached the two young Amazons where they still lay. Hauling first one twin, then the other up on each shoulder, he began making his way toward the exit.

"…Gare…th…"

"Hush now, lass. Save the energy for prayers. We'll need 'em to get the hell outta here before I give out, meself."

"My…Urga…G-grab it…too…?"

"Out of the question, lass! There's no use for it!"

"But I'll…I'll have to take out a…nother loan! T-Tione, help meeee…"

"You seriously better be…joking…"

"Heh. Least you two won't be dyin' anytime soon."

And with that, the three first-tier adventurers, every one of them a sorry sight to behold, left the hall—and the floating remains of the spirit's carcass—behind them.

"Dio Thyrsos!"

Spindles of lightning crackled out of Filvis's wand to incinerate the group of monsters in front of them only a second before the cacophony of footsteps raced down the now-empty passageway toward the surface.

"Aren't we there yet, Lefiya?" Aki called out, supporting one of her injured companions on her shoulder.

"Not much more! It should be…just a little bit farther…!" Lefiya asserted, feeling a trickle of sweat dribble down her temple, probably due to the anxiety she felt.

The party had just about reached its limit, what with the myriad monster and assassin attacks. The frantic desperation of their relentless pursuit seemed almost like a last-ditch attempt to stop them.

"The doors don't seem to be closing anymore. A little weird after the way they were constantly opening and closing before…!" Aki noted as she blocked an incoming attack with her buckler.

"Makes it seem like our enemy's run into somethin' unplanned, too…Whuuaagh!!" Raul fended off the enemy with his longsword, gasping for air along with his comrade.

True enough, none of the enemies appearing before them seemed to be using one of those "keys," almost as though they feared losing them more than anything else. The cause of this was completely

unknown to Raul, Aki, and the rest—that the demi-spirit was causing massive damage to Knossos, and Barca was subsequently pitch-
ing a fit. With the single brain capable of operating Knossos's doors
down for the count, it made their remote control operation essentially impossible.

Those attacking them now were the rest of the Evils, who were
doing everything they could to stop *Loki Familia* from escaping,
though they didn't have the labyrinth's full blessing.

*Mister Gareth and the others still haven't returned... The marks Fil-
vis and I left still remain, but...!*

Again and again, Lefiya glanced behind her with visible apprehension. While Bete and Aiz, at the rear and center of the group,
were currently keeping the enemies at bay, how much longer would
they last? Every one of them was battle-weary and wounded all over,
and their knees threatened to give from the fatigue.

"—! Lefiya!!"

"Huh?!"

The throng of violas appeared without warning from one of the
side passages.

Had someone finally opened a nearby door? The massive flowers,
exclusively used for traps, came at them, attacking friend and foe
alike.

They're too f——!

There was no time. Not for Lefiya's Concurrent Casting. Not for
Filvis's barrier spell.

Drawn to Aiz's wind, the writhing swarm of beasts attacked, and
Lefiya squeezed her eyes shut.

"Wynn Fimbulvetr!"

Only the attack never came, thwarted by a sudden blast of
zero-degree wind.

The white gale froze the entire mob in its spot.

"What...?"

"Don't stop, Lefiya!"

It was Riveria.

And she was already preparing her next spell at the end of the tunnel. Lefiya was speechless for a moment, but at Filvis's urging, she practically tumbled forward, renewing her earlier speed.

They raced past the magic circle currently forming on the ground to find the rest of their companions awaiting their triumphant return.

"Grab the wounded! Hurry!"

"Get them up and outta here—now!"

Alicia and the rest of their old crew extended their hands, yanking the stupefied adventurers forward and out of the maze. Those who couldn't walk were hauled up on shoulders before everyone was taken out, all at once.

"This…Th-this is…" Lefiya stuttered as the rest of her familia bustled around her in ceaseless waves.

"You did well, Lefiya. The staff you left behind—it was the perfect sign." Riveria smiled, not even turning her head as she bombarded the next rush of incoming enemies with her magic. The strategy she'd been using above, utilizing her magic circle as a sort of radar, had detected the rare magic in the magic jewel of Lefiya's staff, and Riveria herself had figured out everything else. She and the rest of the group had used the newly discovered entrance to infiltrate the maze and seek out their companions within.

"Riveria!"

"Are you all right, Aiz?"

"Mister Gareth, Tiona, and Tione…They're still down there…!"

"Our enemy currently lacks leadership. We'll use this opportunity to save them. Gather together those who can still move and find them. We must persevere as long as it takes!"

"Okay!"

"Hey, lady—I'm goin', too!"

As the adventurers reached Riveria's party one after another, Aiz, Bete, Raul, and Aki joined the search-and-rescue effort after some brisk emergency treatment for their wounds.

Lefiya, too, after shaking away her stupor, made to join Aiz. However…

"Lefiya, you will return to the surface."

"B-but, Lady Riveria! I can still move, too! I should go with them...!"

"Says the one severely drained of Mind. I, too, have little power remaining. Leave the efforts to those who can yet fight!" Riveria urged, jade-colored hair clinging to the sweat on her forehead in clumps. Summoning her magic circles again and again for such a powerful spell had drained much of her Mind, to the point where not even her Mind-restoring ability could keep up.

"Lefiya."

"...I know."

Filvis was pulling gently on Lefiya's arm, and Lefiya finally bit down on her lip as she gave the other elf a nod.

Moving away from the rescue party, she and Filvis made their way up the tunnel toward the exit, surrounded on all sides by the protection of their companions. Her lungs were gasping for air now as she ascended that topmost step, but finally, she crossed over the threshold of melting ice and into the freedom beyond.

"...Ah."

In every direction, her wounded companions were being brought to the surface.

Shouts of anger and sorrow formed a storm around her at the sight of their captain.

Tears descended in great, rushing rivers at those they'd been one second too late to save.

The damage the man-made labyrinth Knossos had done was great, and *Loki Familia* had paid a hefty price, but in the end they'd escaped.

"Goddamn...Got away...That slippery blond bastard...Finn..."

The woman, Valletta, wandered the labyrinth's halls in solitude. She was bathed in red from head to toe—blood from the assassins she'd used to wash herself of the monster-attracting powder—making her look very much like a casualty of the carnage herself.

Even after everything, her anger would not be stopped as she tenaciously pursued the prey that had escaped her.

"—Hurry! I hear someone fighting. They must be nearby!"

"...Haaah?"

The bedraggled party crossed her path without warning—one without an arm, one scorched black as though fresh from an explosion, and one weeping bitterly from the pain of untreated wounds. The fact that they were even still alive at all was likely thanks to the healer in glasses following them. She was lending a shoulder to one of her wounded companions, her own face covered in blood as she offered words of encouragement to the rest of the group—even from Valletta's vantage point, it made for a lovely picture.

There was something radiant about her. So devoted. So utterly gallant.

"Leene...it's...fine...Leave me...You need to...get out of here..."

"Please, be strong. It's only a little farther! Just a bit more, and... help will be here!"

And that was why Valletta's thoughts darkened in sadistic glee.

Because what she was about to do next would surely let her see true horror on the face of her mortal enemy.

Yes, how good it would feel to snuff out that glimmering, dazzling light, ahhh—

"Oh-ho-ho..."

Her tongue glided across her bottom lip as she slunk forward, as quiet as a phantom.

"Oh-ho-ho-ho-ho..." Now she was pulling a dagger out of her bloodstained overcoat. Its blade was deep, deep red, imbued with the unimaginable, unadulterated malice of the curse bound to it.

"Hey, kiddos! You're with *Loki Familia*, ain't ya?" she announced, finally revealing herself to the group as her lips curled upward in an impish smile.

"Hmm? Who are—?"

But before the spectacled girl could finish her thought, all she could see was the dagger rushing toward her, accompanied by a high-pitched, carnal laugh.

Blood splattered across the Trickster emblem, coloring it a brilliant vermilion.

Red. So much red.

It stained the inside of his eyes crimson, and it was proof that his consciousness was returning.

"...Ngh."

Wrenching his eyes open, he was met first by the harsh light of the magic-stone lanterns, dim though they were, and he was forced to close them again. The moment his world became dark once more, the unsettling vestiges of reality came crawling back like a dream.

The red returned, so vivid his stomach roiled, and with one last attempt to distance himself from it, he forced his eyes back open.

"Are you awake?" someone asked from just beside him, finally pulling him free of the dream's grasp.

Fighting off a sense of fatigue unlike any he'd ever experienced before, Finn finally opened his eyes.

"...Riveria...Where am I?"

"Dian Cecht's clinic. You've been bedridden since the curse was broken," the mage explained with a candor Finn's sleep-addled mind appreciated.

As for Riveria herself, she'd yet to change from her dirty robes. Accepting only simple treatment, she'd likely been sitting here at his side ever since.

"You've got Amid and the quick-witted efforts of Aki and the others to thank. It came down to the wire, I hear."

The stark white of the sanitized room struck Finn's eyes like dazzling light. He let his gaze travel toward the ceiling as he waited for his surroundings to come into focus...then promptly threw off the sheets, fully prepared to rise to his feet.

"Down, Finn. Back to sleep."

"..."

"Do you even know why I'm here? For exactly this reason. To keep you from leaving this bed."

"..."

"Now, down with you. It's no use masking your true intentions from me," Riveria warned, pointing a finger against the prum's forehead and lightly pressing him back into the comfortable confinement of the bed.

"...I apologize." They had far too much history for him to think he could hide anything from the high elf. "The situation, then...?"

"Last I heard, Aiz and her crew were making ready to withdraw from Daedalus Street. Likely, they've already finished that."

"Then...Gareth and the others?"

"Successfully evacuated. And once everyone was out, all known doors in the labyrinth were closed. There were no signs of pursuit from the enemy."

"...What about casualties?" Finn asked, his voice raspy like that of a sick child.

As he asked this quiet question, sweat beading on his forehead, Riveria's face clouded. Ever so slightly, she averted her eyes.

"There were losses. Seven dead, including those who've gone missing. Lloyd, Crea, Anju, Liza, Kalos, Remilia, and...Leene."

"You all back in one piece, Gareth?"

As the dwarf walked by, Loki asked him a question, gazing out toward the night landscape of the city.

"That I am, ma'am. Right as rain."

"Yer tough as nails; you know that, right?"

They were atop one of the roofs of Daedalus Street. The scarlet-haired goddess was dangling a leg over the edge as she surveyed the dark expanse of the Labyrinth District. Though she didn't turn toward him, Gareth took his place beside her.

"Seems Finn's finally come to."

"Oh? That's good, then."

"Loki."

"Hmm?"

"I'm sorry."

"…"

"For lettin' so many die."

Neither one looked toward the other.

"…Even after all this time, I still don't know how to react when stuff like this happens. I know this ain't our final farewell, so to speak. I'm a god, after all. And part of me gets it."

"Is that so?"

"But…I can't help thinkin' of their faces, y'know? When I'd cop a feel or grab a little ass and they'd get all up in arms. Moments like that, we'll never have again…How do I put it? Feels kinda like losin' yer first love or somethin'."

"I see."

They continued to gaze out across the city.

"Me, I…can't help thinkin' I shoulda shared a few more drinks with 'em."

"You think so…? Yeah…a lot more drinks. Woulda been nice."

They simply peered into the darkness before them with heavy expressions.

"We lost. Those damned orichalcum doors kept me from makin' headway through the maze. Even if I did get the chance to go it again, I don't think the outcome would've change any."

"Those orbs really are the 'key' to everything. At least as far as infiltratin' that place goes."

Their enemy's hideout was truly an impregnable labyrinth. Without a way to move freely through its halls, they couldn't even hope to launch a successful raid. They'd finally had the calamitous "egg" hell-bent on wreaking destruction to the city right under their noses, but they hadn't been able to follow through.

"For now, we'll go seek out info—as well as those keys. Smoke out anything we can find, take any place that seems like it could be connected to those degenerates and turn it upside down."

"Mmn."

"All right! Meeting adjourned. Time to start cookin' our revenge!" Loki suddenly exclaimed, rising to her feet and giving her clothes a quick dusting. Making to leave together with Gareth, she took one last look out across the city. "Wait for us, you shitheads. This war's just beginning," she hissed.

The wrath of Heaven had been released.

Eyes widening, she vowed then and there—Knossos hadn't seen the last of them.

TO BE YEARNED AFTER

Гэта казка іншага сям'і.

Пажадана сур'ёзна; рабіць гэта

Loki Familia put Daedalus Street behind them.

Aiz and the others had come and gone with the rest of Orario none the wiser—barely anyone was even aware of their presence, let alone the battle that had taken place underground in Knossos's hidden passageways. They emerged from the other side with no small amount of injuries and new sacrifices to bear.

The bodies they were able to recover from the labyrinth's halls were buried in the First Graveyard, otherwise known as the Adventurers Graveyard, in the city's southeastern district. Their gravestones would join those of the other adventurers *Loki Familia* had already lost. Tiona, Tione, Lefiya, and others who had been close with the departed wept for them. For a certain golden-haired, golden-eyed swordswoman, however, tears proved yet impossible, and she cursed her own ineptitude as she offered flowers while mourning for the lost souls of her companions.

The familia members who had not yet experienced the pang of death had grown few, nearly all of them bore with them the heartache of friends lost.

And with that anger, they vowed to one day repay the fiends lurking within Knossos in full.

Though the lingering effects of the retreat were still fresh in everyone's minds, aside from a certain skirmish, they were able to return to their normal routines, at least for a short time.

Until, three nights later...

"Nnnnngah! You can't tell me you know where the enemy's lurkin' and then say I shouldn't attack yet! That's just cruel!"

The voice came from the central tower of *Loki Familia*'s home, Twilight Manor, where Loki currently had slovenly kicked up her feet on the desk inside her room on the topmost floor. An aura more disconcerting than even her words surrounded her as she glared off into nothing.

"...And besides that, there's that key. Oh sure, we can look, but where? We've got squat for clues...'cept for ol' Ishtar, who's in cahoots with them and all. She our only option...?"

Considering the assets they had at their disposal, her eyes widened just slightly, and then...

The goddess heard something. A commotion.

"...The hell?"

Straightening up on her chair, she glanced toward the nearby window, only to jump to her feet. She was at the window, eyes opening in startled consternation, then yanking the window open and launching herself from it like some kind of circus acrobat.

In less than a second, she was on the roof.

What drew her attention was the Pleasure Quarter to the city's southeast.

"Is it...on fire?"

The night sky was currently stained a brilliant red from the tendrils of flame.

Loki wasn't the only one to notice it, either. Civilians had halted throughout the streets and were pointing in the direction of the Pleasure Quarter, and even the windows of Twilight Manor were popping open to reveal the half-shocked faces of *Loki Familia* members.

Loki could smell it—the harbinger of war.

She knew then and there that this was no ordinary accident.

"A dispute of some kind? Someone stormin' the lady's keep?"

Ishtar Familia was a prominent familia even among the large organizations of Orario. Though her actual military strength was not too impressive, she had the entirety of the Night District under her control. No one would just up and attack her with no regard for the consequences.

Or, at least, only very few people could manage that, *Loki Familia* included.

"What kinda idiot...?"

But even as the words left her lips, she realized she already knew. A single name rose to the back of her mind.

"Don't tell me…Freya?!"

In an instant, her expression twisted from bewilderment to sheer revulsion. Given Ishtar's open stance of hostility against the other goddess, it could be none other. Loki gave the burning city district a *tch* as she glared into the night sky.

"That idiot's on the move…"

"Th-there's no way…?!"

The world around her had been transformed by flames, screams, and the furtive shadows of incoming assailants. Ishtar found herself at a loss, leaning out over the balcony of her room in her familia's home in mind-numbing shock.

She knew who this was. Only *Freya Familia* could have launched an attack like this on the Pleasure Quarter.

—*She attacked without even waiting for me to strike?*

—*And without a single warning! Preposterous! This is an atrocity!*

She could hear all her preparations, all her plans, coming to nothing—unraveling in an instant.

Reinforcements! I need to get word to Kali in Meren…! But no, the original plan was to launch a pincer attack on Freya's home! To signal them now would be too late! Then should I escape? To Daedalus Street? And unleash the Bull of Heaven? But…oh…ohhh…ohhh-hhhhhhh!! What am I thinking? It's too late now! It's too late to do anything!!

Ishtar's carefully laid plan relied on her being the instigator. To get word to Kali or escape to Knossos would require her to leave the Pleasure Quarter—impossible now that it had already been surrounded.

It was too late. There was nothing she could do.

The moment her enemy had launched a lightning-fast attack, her familia—.

"Freya…?!" the Queen of the Brothel City hissed with a deep-rooted enmity and bloodshot eyes, digging her fingers into the balcony handrail.

"Attack anyone who tries to interfere."
Meanwhile, along the Pleasure Quarter's main street.
The silver-haired Goddess of Beauty walked calmly through the carnage, making her way straight for the temple of Ishtar itself.
"Ishtar may have a short fuse, but she is no fool. She's careful, cunning, not likely to instigate a fight if she knows she's got no chance of winning. From the way she's been acting, she's likely to have an ace up her sleeve..." she murmured to herself, gaze rising as her own followers waged war with the Berbera on both sides of her. Her silver eyes stopped when they reached the temple's balcony and the copper-skinned Goddess of Beauty currently peering over its railing.
Her features twisted into a chilling smile, cold enough to freeze her alluring enemy in place.
"But you've lost."
The true Queen of Beauty was right here.
Ishtar had tried to snatch away the boy she was after, and Freya answered her with an inferno of rage that rivaled the wrath of Heaven itself and razed the carnal district to the ground.

Spectating. Trembling. Trampling.
Though the goddesses played out their respective performances, they shared one common thought between them.
The turmoil besieging them now had been carefully arranged; each of them had been guided toward their actions, almost like some kind of preestablished script.
And Loki remembered someone in particular.
The smile of a certain god rose in her mind.

The center of immoral love was in flames.

Its Amazonian ladies of the night fell one after another in screams of horror that tore through its streets. In the blink of an eye, the Pleasure Quarter of Orario's southeastern district, along with its adventurers, fighting beneath the emblem of the warring maiden, was obliterated from the map.

A certain god narrowed his eyes watching the scene of carnage amid the red embers wafting into the night air.

"Just how much of this was according to plan?" Behind Hermes, Asfi Al Andromeda asked a question that brought a smile to his lips. "This was your goal, then? The downfall of *Ishtar Familia*?" she asked again, knowing all too well the evasive nature of her enigmatic patron deity.

Just as he'd said he would after Ishtar's name had come up during his investigations with Loki and Dionysus, Hermes had "done his work properly." The tempest of Ishtar's jealousy had simply gone too far, and he'd judged her capable of bringing about Orario's ruin. Thus, he'd set to work in secret, using his connections as a neutral familia, Ishtar's undiluted rage toward Freya, as well as Freya's "treasure" to sow the proper seeds.

Then those seeds had blossomed.

They gave way to a magnificent, dazzling, sensational bloom of fire and destruction.

"For your own personal gratification? Or perhaps...a test of sorts?"

Asfi's next question was right on the money.

Hermes just smiled. "Humans...gods...even that one girl; we're all looking for the same thing. No one is different."

The blazing red Pleasure Quarter.

The spectacle of fire and brimstone as the violent battle ensued.

And the single boy, fighting on and on in its midst.

Hermes's gaze took everything in as he spoke.

"The world seeks its hero."

The One-Eyed Dragon—the last of the Three Great Quests.

And the equally as formidable menace—the demi-spirit, recently discovered.

Having left behind the Dungeon, the mother of all this, the darkness now encroached on the city, writhing and squirming as the footsteps of devastation echoed right outside its doors.

The crisis was already at hand.

"We still don't have enough pawns. Yes...we need our Joker," he murmured, his voice joining the rising embers on the breeze.

They were all watching the Pleasure Quarter now.

"A brilliant white light...that can cut through the darkness."

The shadowy Labyrinth District and its denizens of the deep.

"A chiming bell...that will save the chosen ones."

The golden-haired, golden-eyed maiden in her soaring tower in the city's northern district.

"The last hero...who can bear the Era of Promise on his shoulders."

Yes, the gazes of everyone in the entire city had converged on a single battlefield, where the first cries of new warriors ascended to the heavens.

And in a vague, nebulous, self-righteous, and almost desperate prophecy, Hermes delivered his oracle.

"For the sake of the world's deepest, most primordial wish... I will——"

Gareth · Landrock

BELONGS TO:	Loki Familia		
RACE:	Dwarf	JOB:	adventurer
DUNGEON RANGE:	fifty-ninth floor	WEAPONS:	ax, hammer, greatsword
CURRENT WORTH:	66,450,000 valis		

Status

Lv.6

STRENGTH:	S 997	ENDURANCE:	S 996
DEXTERITY:	D 564	AGILITY:	E 489
MAGIC:	H 117	PUMMEL:	E
MAGIC RESISTANCE:	E	IMMUNITY:	G
FRACTURE:	H	BULWARK:	H

MAGIC:	Earth Raid	• Earth-destructive magic. • Power directly correlates to Strength stat. • Can be cast only while on the ground.
SKILLS:	Dvergr Enhance	• Raises Strength stat.
	Ardigalea	• Raises Endurance stat. • Raises resistance to attack magic.

EQUIPMENT: **Grand Ax**

• A large battle-ax. Gareth's main weapon.
• Crafted by Tsubaki of Hephaistos Familia for around 45,000,000 valis (price fluctuates).
• A first-tier weapon provided at a reasonable cost thanks to the direct contract he's forged with the Master Smith.
• Every time it breaks from Gareth's excessive strength, Tsubaki is mortified and crafts him a new, stronger battle-ax.
• Due to Gareth's contract (decree) with Tsubaki, he's not allowed to use any weapon not of Tsubaki's making.

EQUIPMENT: **Roland Ax**

• Durandal weapon.
• One of the "Roland Series" weapons crafted by Tsubaki.
• A great ax with markedly lower power than that of Gareth's Grand Ax.
• 10,000,000 valis.

GARETH LANDROCK

Afterword

I hit a (dare I say) crisis like no other while working on this book. Originally, I'd hoped to provide a sort of behind-the-scenes look at the happenings of the seventh book in the main series—what happens to our hero on his way back after being forced to spend the night in the Pleasure Quarter. The Sword Princess and her companions would have run into him on their own way back from the Labyrinth District, whereby a certain fairy heroine would have caught whiff of his red-light-district musk, prompting another bout of rage-induced pursuit around the city that results in disaster. This would eventually lead to my two main characters getting another chance alone together. A sort of romantic-comedy scene would have ensued where the Sword Princess would have acted distant and formal, misunderstanding why the white rabbit was mumbling about a prostitute. With a little bit of luck and Bell's knowledge of the epic, they would then have discovered the enemy's stronghold, infiltrated the labyrinth together with our fairy heroine and the rest of the group, leading to Aiz and Bell running into Levis, which would have instigated their first joint battle, along with other various happenings, until finally, after separating from the rest of the group, a number of life-saving circumstances would have resulted in their first kiss...That was the tentative outline I had written, at least, though it was mostly just some ideas I jotted down.

However, after meeting with my editors, we reached the conclusion that "it would simply be unreasonable to include Bell," what with the inconsistencies this could create with the already published main series. My prepared plot was then thrown out the window, and no matter how much I screamed and put up a fight, I still had the deadline looming on the horizon, thus forcing me to "think and write," basically ad-libbing the entire book (a new challenge for me).

It was tough, but somehow, I managed to make decent headway. Until the fated day arrived.

The last day of my deadline: and somehow, the coup de grâce, the final battle, was unwritten.

It wasn't that I didn't know how to depict it but rather that I didn't even know what to depict! It was like setting out on an adventure without a map—terrifying, let me tell you—and with grim despair, I reluctantly took up the reins of the bitter legacy I'd left myself in the cliffhanger from the previous book, the Bull of Heaven...but even then, I was soon to be at my wits' end.

I didn't have my elves with their rule-defying, last-ray-of-hope-type magic, and even Braver was knocked out...Yes, it turned out having nothing but a dwarf and two Amazons didn't leave me with many options at all...I was doomed! The end was nigh...!

At this rate, I was going to have to accept the risks and revise what I'd written to throw the Sword Princess and the werewolf into the mix...! Only then, just as I was about to move forward with the forbidden act, my characters, quite literally, broke.

Huh? Tug-of-war? Seriously? Is this okay?

Is there even a demand for these guys?

Oh, who cares! Look at their passion! Go, go, go, goooooooo! Get 'em!

Huuuuwwwwoooooouuuuugggghhhh! GOLDION HAMMERRR!!

...Which is seriously how it went down those last few nights: my brain was warped by zero sleep and pure, unadulterated fear.

I was too scared to even reread the last half of the book. So I'll have to leave it up to you, my readers, to decide if the final takedown was even within the realms of plausibility or not. As for me, I mostly just realized that I suck at ad-libbing...

At any rate, let's move on to my words of thanks for this volume.

To my editors, Otaki and Takahashi, as well as chief editor Kitamura, I apologize sincerely for the slew of hard-won battles this side series has become. It would be nice if the next book could finally be a bit of a respite. Also to my illustrator, Kiyotaka Haimura, I tip my hat at the brilliant way you depicted nearly all my enemy characters.

As this volume will also be released as a limited edition, I'd like to additionally thank Waki Ikawa for the pamphlet illustrations, as well as Takashi Yagi for his continued work on the manga version being released by Gangan Joker. Seeing my work come alive in the form of illustrations and comics brings me such joy. I want to thank both of you from the bottom of my heart. To everyone else who helped make this book possible, I also extend my thanks. And, of course, to you as well, my dear readers, who have stayed by my side all this time.

This book ended up having a number of scenes that pained me to write, which only added to overall fatigue. For this reason, I'm thinking the next book might be a story about a certain werewolf—no, it must! He may be a *tsundere* (is that the right word?), but he needs a chance to shine, or howl in this case, and I hope you'll stick with me for it.

Those who've read my ramblings all the way till the end—thank you. All the best.

Fujino Omori